THE
KING
AND HIS
AGENTS

THE
KING
AND HIS
AGENTS

DONATO J. DAVIS

ARCHWAY
PUBLISHING

Archway Publishing books may be ordered through booksellers or by contacting:

Archway Publishing
1663 Liberty Drive
Bloomington, IN 47403
www.archwaypublishing.com
844-669-3957

ISBN: 978-1-6657-4198-9 (sc)
ISBN: 978-1-6657-4199-6 (e)

Library of Congress Control Number: 2023906696

Print information available on the last page.

Archway Publishing rev. date: 04/03/2023

CONTENTS

1

THE LEADER

WHAT MAKES A GREAT LEADER? Is it strength? Respecting the people? Solving every problem? Ruling with an iron fist, or taking a more democratic approach? The truth is there is no one clear answer to that question. There is no one way to lead, every man has their leadership style. Not every man is born to lead, some are better at it than others. But for better or worse, leaders who are memorialized for eternity within the pages of history books have exhibited certain common attributes that helped them create their legacies. Every leader must be strong-minded, ambitious, have confidence, charisma, command respect, and can inspire those around them. They must possess vision, great poise, and be skilled in handling issues that arise. And perhaps most importantly, they must be surrounded by the right group of people that can aid in assuring their success.

Those are the basic ingredients that every leader must possess. Afterward, they can add all their personal qualities to help put a face on their reign. But no face disgusted me more than that of the President of San Diamo, Fredicio DeOrtiz. DeOrtiz came to power seven years ago off the old promise to bring prosperity to the people of San Diamo.

He played us for fools. The greedy, womanizing, self-serving, incompetent, power-hungry, liar ended up driving the once proud nation of San Diamo into the ground. An utter disgrace. Corruption was rampant and the economy was decimated. Most of the money that should've been going towards the benefit of the people was instead going towards bribes and paying off some DeOrtiz's wealthy friends and family members. Some of whom he gave positions of power within the government though they had no business being there. Moreover, the horrendous mismanagement of the government caused the economy to collapse, millions of people were out of work, banks failed, essential services such as healthcare and policing were in insufficient supply, crime was out of control, and food and money were becoming scarce. Millions of people were plunged into poverty and on the brink of starvation, and to make matters worse; DeOrtiz was determined to hang on to power at all costs.

San Diamo was in complete disarray. It was a ticking time bomb just nearing the end of its final countdown and just waiting to detonate. But maybe, just maybe, an explosion isn't such a bad thing. Maybe the bomb does need to go off and rid the people of San Diamo of its so-called "leaders". Maybe what is needed, is revolution. And sure enough, the bomb finally did explode. Two months ago, in the early spring, the anger of the people had finally boiled over. How fitting. Spring is the season of change and rebirth, and San Diamo's rebirth had arrived at last.

The nation's poor and those who have been hurt and forgotten under DeOrtiz's disastrous administration took to the streets of the capital city Tipedre in the early morning of April 6, 1984, to demand one thing only; that DeOrtiz steps down peacefully or be removed by force. The morning was cool and calm, but the thunderous voices of the angry masses added a dissonance that was impossible to not recognize. Thousands upon thousands of people from all walks of life and from across the country gathered at the doorsteps of the congress house and the presidential office to voice their long-held frustrations. The crowds were so thick that it was virtually impossible to walk through. I guess it's true what they say, protest is the voice of the unheard.

The crowds raised their voice in unison and chanted "¡limpia la escoria!" ("clean the wood") and "¡el tirano debe irse!" (The tyrant must go!). However, the loudness of the chants paled in comparison to how deafening the expressions of anger and resentment were on the people's faces that day. The image of years of suffering was painted so vividly. Da Vinci himself may not have been able to capture it. My heart ached immensely that day. Unfortunately for me, I was on a different side of the coin that day. When leaders feel as if their power is being threatened, they resort to one of two options. Peaceful appeasement or responding with brute force. To a surprise to no one, DeOrtiz chose the latter. To maintain his grip on power, DeOrtiz ordered that the military immediately step in and disperse the crowds by any means necessary. A simple request seeing as most of the top officials in the military, and DeOrtiz were close friends. This is where I come into the picture.

I was a young private back then. Private Juan Santano. I had joined the army just three months prior and this was my first time experiencing any kind of action. I had always thought that the first time I would ever have to use a weapon was overseas or while defending the country from foreign invaders. I would've never imagined that my first taste of duty would be against my countrymen. Our orders that day were to aid the overwhelmed local law enforcement in dispersing the crowds and restoring order to the streets of Tipedre. I remember standing in the front lines behind a police barricade in front of two military armored trucks as we guarded the presidential mansion that was directly behind us. We were fully armed with rubber bullets, tear gas, gas masks, riot shields, batons, and flashbangs. The good Lord knows that my heart and my conscience were not in agreement with using force against the people. I sympathized with them. I felt their anger, their pain, their frustration. I felt the bite of poverty and suffered from the venom of not being able to provide for my family. It was why I joined the army in the first place. I stood there enduring the turmoil that was within me. Knowing that I must stand with the people against the DeOrtiz regime but also grappling with the fact that disobeying orders in the military is seen as treason and is punishable by death.

The fury of the people grew with every passing minute. As they pushed against the barricades, they hurled all manner of projectiles such as stones and whatever else they could find toward us. They called us "¡traidores!" (traitors!) and "¡peones!" (pawns!). Many of them used more explicit words to vent their anger. The atmosphere grew increasingly tense. It was like scorching hot steam was emanating from the people and sweeping across Tipedre. They were no longer here to scream at DeOrtiz and hope that he'd fold to their demands and leave. No, they wanted his head. And if it were up to me, I'd gladly give it to them. Yet, there I was defending the coward as he hid inside the mansion.

The barricades were not going to hold the angry mob back forever. Within any minute, they would subside, and the mob would begin their stampede into the mansion. However, a final plea was made before the chaos unfolded.

"Citizens, please leave this area immediately and return to your homes! This will be your only warning! Return to your homes immediately or else we will have to use force!"

That voice was coming from the rear of the formation. I looked behind me and there he was standing so stoically on the staircase of the mansion. One hand behind his back and the other holding a megaphone up to his lips to ensure that his commands were heard. Lieutenant Louis Caesar. He was a made- man in the military who carried a reputation of speaking softly while carrying a big stick. He had served in the army for nearly two decades, garnering the respect and admiration of all the men under his command. The perfect combination of intelligence and vigor, he could win the battle of the mind and weapons if needs be. Any man would gladly follow him into battle and have hope that they would make it home alive. His very presence exhumed strength, honor, and valor. He was the perfect soldier. Yet, I was conflicted about him. How could a man of such high prestige serve in an army that is filled with puppets of one of the vile men who ever walked the earth? How could he go along with defending such a man and find comfort in using force against his people? Is he really who he says he is?

My questions would have to receive their answers at another time. The patience of the mob had finally worn thin, and their anger had now boiled over. They managed to topple the barricades and make their way toward us with a fierce charge. I immediately put on my gas mask, drew my baton with one hand, and placed my riot shield in front of me with the next. It was as if I was at war in medieval times. For a moment, it felt as though time had slowed. I could feel my heart pounding in my chest, and my breathing became deeper yet, shorter at the same time. I tried to keep an unperturbed demeanor but unfortunately was unable to. My hands and knees couldn't stop shaking. I knew I was on the wrong side of this fight. Perhaps if I was a part of the mob, I would have a lion's will to fight; but there I was just waiting to hear the order from Lieutenant Caesar. And then it came.

"Advance!" yelled the lieutenant through the megaphone.

And in one mighty charge, I and the rest of the soldiers that were there with me that day brawled in the streets of Tipedre with our fellow countrymen. The pride of the San Diamo army was tainted for eternity. The carnage was unlike anything that I had ever seen before in my lifetime. The only thought that invaded my mind during the madness of the riot was if this was the beginning of a civil war? Instead of rubber bullets, would I soon have to use live rounds on my brothers and sisters? I was ashamed, horrified, and deeply saddened. My heart wept for San Diamo. Something had to be done to rid this country of this curse. Fortunately, I would find an answer soon enough.

2

MEETING IN SECRET

IT TOOK SIX HOURS FOR us to regain control of the streets of Tipedre. It was just past 5 PM and the sun was beginning to set. The air was stained with the scent of tear gas, rubber bullets littered every inch of the ground beneath my feet, and my ears were still ringing from the sound of exploding flashbangs. A few of the surrounding buildings were destroyed by fires caused by Molotov cocktails that few protesters were using. A few other buildings were looted. We managed to disperse most of the crowds with the aid of water cannons that the military had at their disposal for routine training exercises. Many of the protesters were arrested by law enforcement. Other protesters along with some police officers and army members were wounded, and a few died. Tipedre was a dead ghost town that night. If you didn't know any better, you would have believed that you had entered the remains of a war zone.

The exhaustion I felt that night was more than words could describe. But I couldn't go home to lay beside my wife, Eliza, and children Maria and Julio. While walking alone through the streets feeling drained and bruised from the events that had taken place that day, I came into an alleyway and overheard DeOrtiz's address to the nation that was being played from a radio that sat upon an open window of a house nearby. In his address, DeOrtiz announced a state of emergency, and that the military was to patrol the streets to keep the peace. It was also announced that a nationwide 7:00 PM curfew would be implemented for the next two weeks, and any citizen seen out past that time would be detained.

I leaned against a wall with a viper's head graffiti art on it. I held my head hung down in utter fatigue. Suddenly, I became drenched with blistering cold water. I looked up at the window where the radio was and saw a woman with a small bucket in one hand and her small son clutched to her side in the next. A boy that appeared to be almost as young as my son. You could see the poor boy's ribs peeking from behind his flesh clear as day. A clear sign that he hasn't had much to eat recently. A painful reminder of the harsh reality that many people in San Diamo had to face daily. I said nothing to the woman, I could only stare at her and become broken by the look of pure disgust she had in her eyes as she stared back at me.

"¡Títere del diablo!" ("devil's puppet!"), the woman called me as I turned around to carry on my walk of shame.

Her words pierced deep, but I couldn't complain because I could understand where she was coming from. That was life in San Diamo these days, no one trusted anyone. Not their neighbors, their friends, not even the blood of their family members. Trust was only something you did if you wanted to end up disappointed, or perhaps dead.

As the night sky began to set in, my wandering across the city brought me to the square. I always considered it the most beautiful part of the city. It always had a charming aesthetic. Brick roads, candlelit streetlamps, and the massive cathedral that overlooked the coast were all tied together with a lovely fountain with water so refreshing that you could bathe in it. I was alone in the square, which was fine by me; I needed solitude. I stopped for a drink of water from the fountain and once my thirst was quenched, I then proceeded to make my way to the cathedral. As I entered the yard, there was a statue of the Virgin Mary standing in its center. I walked up to the statue and briefly admired it.

"I pray that your son will forgive me and that he will deliver us from this evil," I said rather repentantly to the statue.

I then sat on the steps of the cathedral, laid my head back, stared into the night sky for a while, and shut my eyes. A few minutes had passed, then suddenly I heard a voice.

"Statues can't hear you; you know," said the voice.

I immediately opened my eyes and looked up to see a soldier smoking a cigarette standing in front of me. He reeked with the smell of tear gas, and he had a soulless look in his eyes; probably because he was tired from what had transpired earlier. His face was covered with dirt and sweat, and his stoic facial expression was well-complemented by his rough and jagged beard. You would think that a soldier would look more groomed, but I suppose given the circumstances, everyone had a right to look like they had seen better days.

"Who are you?" I asked since he wasn't wearing his name patch.

"That's not important right now," he replied with a snarky. "I only have one question for you."

I stared at the stranger for a bit, and I was tempted to draw my gun and attack him. He wouldn't tell me his name, I didn't even know where he came from, and I wasn't about to drop my guard for a single second. I began to slowly reach for my firearm but before I could finish, his was pointing right at my head.

"Go ahead and draw your gun," he said. "I'll give you two choices though. Either answer my question or draw your weapon and die right here on the cathedral steps. Your choice."

I looked him straight in his eyes when he spoke, and I could see that if I made the wrong choice, he would make good on his threat and leave a bullet in my head. I slowly receded my hands from my side and raised them to my head in surrender.

"What's your question?" I asked him.

He kept his pistol at my head, took another draw of his cigarette, and said,

"I heard you asking the statue there for God's help to deliver San Diamo. But God only helps those who help themselves. Do you want to help save San Diamo?"

I paused for a minute as I considered his question. My heart was pounding in my chest and sweat was dripping down my face, I didn't know what to say to him. All I knew at that moment was that I was staring down the barrel of a gun and depending on my answer, he may pull the trigger without giving it a second thought. He stood above me silently as he waited for a response. I took another minute to think, then finally, I gave my answer.

"Yes. I do," I said while panting.

"Good," he answered in a soft tone as he put his weapon away.

The mysterious man then turned around and took one more puff of his cigarette before finally dropping it on the ground and crushing it beneath his boot.

"Follow me," he instructed before proceeding to walk out of the yard into the square.

I slowly got up from the cathedral steps and began following the man. We walked through the city for nearly an hour, pretending to be on duty as we passed other troops on patrol. He led me to an avenue in the southern end of the city that was lit by a single streetlight. To my suspicion, there were no patrol units as far as the eye could see. This part of the city had a reputation for being deep in poverty and overran with crime. I had my reservations as to why we would venture off into this part of the city so late at night, but I didn't ask. I just obediently followed this strange man who pointed a gun at my head not too long ago into a place where I could very likely have my throat slit. How wise of me. It was past 9 PM and we eventually came to an abandoned warehouse. I could see that lights were turned on inside and I could hear the voices of people as well. I thought to myself that it was past curfew and people should be in their homes right now, but then again, no one cared about the law anymore.

The man knocked on the door and was greeted by its slight opening. The voice on the other side said, "¿Pasaporte?" ("Passport?")

The man then rolled up his right sleeve and revealed a tattoo of a viper's head on his forearm to show to the person on the other side of the door. The door opened and as we entered, the man stopped for a moment and told the person who opened the door that I was a "new recruit" and that it was alright for me to come in. The man obliged and as I walked inside, I stood for a minute to analyze the room. It was filled with fellow soldiers, and men and women both young and old who all looked as if they were prepared to kill a man at a moment's notice. The room felt heavy as I walked through it still following the man from the cathedral. I was greeted by side glances and looks of skepticism. I noticed that everyone in the room had the same viper head tattoo on their right forearm. What was this place? And who were these people?

Suddenly, the man from the cathedral threw his hand around me and pulled me close.

"Stay calm and don't do anything to get yourself killed. We'll be starting the meeting soon," he whispered into my ear.

I followed him to a makeshift bar that was in the corner of the warehouse. He sat on a stool at the counter, and I took a seat next to him. He requested a glass of tequila on ice from the bartender. I, on the other hand, didn't have anything to drink. I looked across the room and saw a makeshift stage with a pulpit in its center. This was all strange. What was the meaning behind all this? Just what was I being "recruited" for? I needed answers, and I was going to get them. I quickly drew my pistol and held it to the side of the man's head He didn't look at me. He just continued to sit there having his drink, completely unbothered by a pistol being pointed at his head. He chuckled.

"You must be a damn fool to do something like that in a room like this," he said while taking a sip of his drink.

I looked up at the bartender and saw him slowly lift his shirt to reveal the gun he was concealing behind his belt. A subtle yet stern warning. For the second time that night, I was intimidated into not using my weapon. I slowly put my gun back into its holster, but I did not hold my silence.

"So, what are we doing here?" I asked the man from the cathedral.

"I told you, we're here for a meeting,"

"A meeting about what?" I asked, determined to receive an answer.

The man kept sipping his drink and insisted on not revealing any substantial details about what was to take place or why he brought me here.

"Relax," he said firmly. "You'll understand once he arrives."

It was pointless. The secretive soldier whose name I didn't know yet, who I was entrusting with my life left me with more questions than answers. I sighed in frustration.

"Could you at least tell me your name?" I asked him.

"Hector. Hector Valdez," he answered as he took a shot of what has left of his drink.

As soon as he had put his glass on the counter, the doors of the warehouse opened once more, and in came three soldiers. One wearing dark tinted glasses and the other two following closely behind him with rifles in hand as if they were his bodyguards. My intuition told me that there was something familiar about the one wearing the glasses, but I just couldn't put my finger on it. The mysterious, shaded macho-man made his way up towards the small makeshift stage and stood behind the pulpit. Both soldiers who came with him stood at opposing ends of the stage at its base. While this was happening everyone else in the room began to gather in front of the stage and stood quietly. It was like a congregation waiting to hear the preacher deliver his sermon. Hector and I got up from where we were. Hector made his way onto the stage, standing at attention behind the militant pastor. I took my place amongst the audience, and I began to wonder if I had stumbled into a cult for a moment. The room grew silent. Everyone around me was waiting in earnest anticipation for the man at the pulpit to begin speaking.

"Buenas Noches, camaradas," (Good night my comrades) he politely greeted the audience.

Then, in a moment of shock, the man standing at the pulpit slowly raised his hands to his face to remove his glasses and reveal his identity.

As his glasses came off his face, my jaw inched ever closer to touching the floor. I was in utter disbelief. As if I was not already perplexed by what was happening, that moment only added to my questions. I now felt as if I was nearing the point of insanity. The man at the pulpit that night was Lieutenant Caesar.

3

INSPIRING WORDS

LIEUTENANT CAESAR, WHAT WAS A man like him doing in a place like this? The strange night became even more unusual. From that point, I had no longer found anything surprising. The lieutenant was preparing to give a speech of some sort, and I knew that the only way that I would gain any answers, any form of clarity and reason as to what was happening; was by listening. A grave silence fell upon the room, and finally, the lieutenant spoke.

"My fellow patriots!" he bellowed. "I know you're all still shaken, perhaps even angered by what has happened today in the capital. It was horrendous and due to these circumstances, many of our members could not be here with us tonight."

He went on by saying, "but make no mistake, this is just a fore-shadowing of what is to come if we continue to let this oppressive government, our enemies, stand on our necks any longer. When you are being provoked, you are well within your rights to fight back against your provocateurs until the abuse stops, or else; you will continue to be mistreated by those who see you as having less dignity than animals. However, perhaps they are right. We are animals, we are a beast that is to be feared. A beast that moves with stealth and kills with proficiency. This is why we exist! We are the ones who must bring corrupt power to justice! We are the ones who must shine a light on what lives in the shadows! We are the ones who must rise! We are the ones who must use righteous anger to purge San Diamo of this evil! We are the ones who must usher in a new era! We are the liberators! WE. ARE. THE. VIPERS!"

The audience echoed back the word "vipers" like a choir adding harmony to the lead singer's vocals. They loved the lieutenant's message and endorsed every word that left his mouth. He spoke with such passion, such conviction, such charisma, such intelligence, such persuasion; you could tell that his heart was burning with every word and the flames consumed the hearts of all those who were there that night to hear it. You could feel his words seeping into the cracks of frustration and resentment that laid upon the hearts and minds of everyone in the room and making them whole. It was an odd feeling, but the lieutenant had my attention and he commanded it at his will.

In his speech, he railed against DeOrtiz and his corrupt allies in the government and he held them responsible for "poisoning" San Diamo with their agenda to serve themselves rather than working to the benefit of the people. He blasted the wealthy elitist class and blamed their greed and selfishness for the cause of San Diamo's desolation and the suffering of the common folk. Seeing them as the "enemy of the people" who must "lose as much as they gain if San Diamo is to prosper". Caesar was right. They were the people who had the power to do better for San Diamo, but they instead chose to see the country and its less fortunate rot while they were in pursuit of their selfish ambitions to bathe themselves in wealth and power. Every inch of the blame rested at their feet. Caesar proposed one simple cure for this cancer, revolution, by any means necessary. Toppling the greedy establishment led by DeOrtiz and building a new San Diamo from the rubble.

"Who is to help us if we don't help ourselves?" he asked. A question to which I and everyone there that night knew the answer. No one.

I agreed with every word that Caesar had said. They were accurate and they spoke the words which the hearts of everyone there that night could not say. It was as though he glanced into our souls and gave voice to the voiceless. I was overwhelmed, but, in a good way. I felt tears in my eyes; I felt understood and as though I was heard without saying a word. I felt something that I had not felt in such a long time, I felt hope. And given how the rest of the audience gave cheers of adulation, thunderous rounds of applause, and showed unwavering support for the lieutenant; I knew they felt the same.

Before the lieutenant wrapped up the hour-long speech, he rolled up his right sleeve to reveal the same viper head tattoo on his forearm which he then raised with a fist in the air and yelled, "viper!". The audience, including myself, followed suit though I was without the tattoo. The lieutenant then descended the stage with Hector to the resounding cheers and applause of those in attendance. I was moved by the speech, and I believed that I had found my destiny. God himself orchestrated this night for a reason. Who was I to question him?

My heart was convinced but my mind still had one obstacle it needed to pass before I could commit myself to join the lieutenant's cause. What the lieutenant was doing by giving a speech like this was blatant sedition and if I went along with his plans to overthrow DeOrtiz, both I and everyone in this room could be executed for treason. How did I know that the lieutenant wasn't just a part of a government plot to capture those who opposed DeOrtiz? How could I be sure that those powerful words weren't only the bait that was being used to lure myself and everyone else into a trap? After all, the lieutenant did order and sit idly by as the soldiers brutalized the very same people, he was claiming to now be a champion of earlier in the day. There were other soldiers there, how could I trust them? Besides, DeOrtiz did have most of the military in his pockets. This could all just be a trick of smoke and mirrors that ends with my blood being spilled. I looked across the room and saw the lieutenant standing in a corner speaking with Hector and two other soldiers. I wanted answers, and nothing would stand in my way of receiving them.

"Lieutenant Sir, may I speak with you for a moment?" I requested.

"You're getting on my last nerve!" Hector said in a fit of anger as he drew his gun at me.

"Hector!" said the lieutenant firmly. "Put it down."

Hector did as he was told and put his weapon down without another word. The lieutenant didn't even have to look at him.

"Leave us," the lieutenant then ordered.

Hector and the other two soldiers immediately took their leave.

"You must forgive the corporal. He can be a little 'hot-headed' at times but trust me, he is a good man. One of the best I have."

"Yes sir, I am well aware," I replied.

"Please, call me Caesar. Would you care for a drink private?" he said in a gentle tone.

This was a far cry from what I had just witnessed from Lieutenant Caesar. The man who was giving that fiery speech not too long ago had now suddenly evolved within the span of just a few short minutes. He was incredibly polite and respectful, showing great poise and a gentleman's elegance in his demeanor. Yet, he carried a reputation of being a cold-blooded killer within the army. His reputation exceeded him. He did speak softly and carried a big stick. He was most definitely a viper in human skin, though, one could make the argument that he may also be a poisonous dart frog that simply changes its colors to match its surroundings. One drives more fear in you than the other, but they're both equally deadly. And for that reason, I was hesitant in trusting him.

Nonetheless, I agreed to have a drink with Caesar, and I followed him towards the makeshift bar. He sat down to a glass of tequila while I enjoyed some American whiskey.

"What is your name private?" he asked me.

"Juan Santano," I answered.

"It's a pleasure to meet you, Juan," he said as he shook my hand. "Where are you from?"

"Capacha," I replied.

"Ah yes, the farmlands. It's beautiful out there, especially at this time of year,"

Caesar and I spent some time making small talk and getting to know each other. He asked me about my family, and we talked about what made us join the army. I told him that DeOrtiz's policy of forcibly evicting and selling small family farms to large produce supplying businesses to "boost employment" drove families such as mine into poverty. We lost everything and that was why I had moved to Tipedre with my wife and children. So that we could find work. I joined the army because I heard that the wages were good. Until of course, DeOrtiz's administration cut the salaries of soldiers. Caesar expressed that he joined the army because that was his dream as a child. He admitted that he took pride in serving his country but that all changed when DeOrtiz cut the salaries of soldiers and gave raises to higher-ranking army officers to buy their loyalty. Caesar, with tears in his eyes, told me that his daughter eventually fell ill and without the money needed to purchase her medication, she passed away and hence why he founded the Vipers. My heart sunk at his story.

Caesar wiped his eyes, and the conversation eventually came to the meat of the matter, and I was going to make the most of the opportunity.

"Your speech was impressive," I complimented. "But there is something I must ask you."

"And what might that be?" he asked.

"Did you mean everything that you said in your speech?"

"What do you mean?" he inquired.

"I want you to convince me. You spoke as if you were willing to help the people, but you were fine with us fighting against them in the streets earlier today. You had the opportunity to take DeOrtiz down. Why didn't you?"

He held his head down and sighed as if he was feeling regret, then took a sip of his drink.

"I am not proud of what happened," he said. "I am quite ashamed of it. However, it was necessary. Tell me, Juan, have you ever read about the city of Troy?"

"I'm not familiar with it,"

He paused for a minute and then proceeded to tell the story of the Trojan war. An epic tale, where according to ancient Greek mythology, there was a war between the city of Troy and the Greeks after the Trojan prince Paris took princess Helen away from her husband Menelaus - king of Sparta. Menelaus was angered and he, along with his brother Agamemnon gathered a large Greek army to wage war against Troy to get his wife back. Troy, however, was an impregnable city, and the Greeks struggled while laying siege to it. The war, however, came to a decisive end after the Greeks devised a plan to construct a massive wooden horse that was hollow on the inside. The horse was a sacred animal to the Trojans and since the Greek army had abandoned their camps, the Trojans saw this wooden horse as a gift from the gods and brought the horse into the city to celebrate Troy's victory over the Greeks.

"Little did the people of Troy know that some of the Greek soldiers were hiding inside the horse," Caesar said with a gleaming look in his eyes. "And when night came, the soldiers exited the horse, slaughtered the people of Troy and burned the city to the ground."

"So, you're saying that you're the horse?" I asked.

He looked me straight in my eyes. "I knew you were a wise man, Juan. Yes, I am the Trojan horse."

I understood what Caesar was trying to say. He was acting as the Trojan horse so that DeOrtiz and his allies would fall into a false sense of security before striking the death blow. That's why he did what he had done. I was intrigued and I wanted to learn more. I asked Caesar about Viper and he told me that the organization had networks across San Diamo, and they were lying in wait for the moment they would launch their revolution and free the country from DeOrtiz's clutches once and for all.

"Juan, now that you know all this, will you lend your strength to our cause?" he asked in a soft tone. "Everyone in this room has suffered immensely at the hands of this monster. Please help us bring him to justice."

He stretched his hand towards me so that we could shake hands in agreement. I looked at his outstretched hand for a moment and as

I sat pondering his question and recalling all of what had occurred throughout the day. It was clear that there was only one clear choice. I was no longer indecisive; I had now been convinced. DeOrtiz had to be removed and it would be the honor of a lifetime to know that I would be doing my country a great service by participating in doing so. I looked directly into his eyes and without any further thought, I firmly shook Caesar's hand. I received the viper head tattoo on my right forearm to make our contract official.

"Welcome to the Vipers, Juan," Caesar said, pleased.

I too was pleased that night, I had found a new calling and San Diamo's salvation was now on the horizon. I was a liberator. I was a viper.

4

PLAN OF ACTION

TWO WEEKS HAD PASSED SINCE the meeting at the warehouse. Since then, I have been spending my time between being on patrol and seeing my family whenever I get the chance. I was anxious to know the next time that I would meet with the Vipers. Our meetings had to remain discreet to avoid any unwanted attention to our operation. Caesar, as the leader, spent the time acting out his usual role as the Trojan horse. And he was playing his role to perfection by getting close to top military officials and even DeOrtiz himself. Providing the enemy with a false sense of security while plotting their inevitable demise. A genius and lethal strategy.

It was just after 6:00 PM and I was preparing to leave home for the night to go on curfew patrol. I hadn't told Eliza about my involvement with Viper due to my desire to ensure her safety and that of our children. In case anything was to go wrong, keeping them at a distance would be the wisest thing to do. Eliza did interrogate me as to when I received the viper head tattoo on my forearm. I, unfortunately, had to lie to my beloved wife and tell her that it was just a welcome gift from some of my friends in the army. Though I wasn't proud to be concealing information like this from my family, I knew that it would all one day be worth it when they live in a better San Diamo. They will all understand in due time. Besides, what was marriage without the occasional white lies?

I gave my children a warm embracing hug before I left, gave my wife an affectionate kiss on the cheek; then made my way through the door. As I stepped into our dark, backwater neighborhood; I stepped on something that felt as if it was paper. I looked down and saw that I was standing on what appeared to be a card. I picked it up and saw the viper's head with the words "Warehouse, 9 PM" written on it. Though I was greatly uneased that this message arrived at my home without me disclosing where I reside to anyone within Viper, I was also elated that another meeting was approaching. My intuition told me that there was something of utmost importance to be discussed.

My hours on patrol were long and rather dull. Perhaps because I was eagerly waiting for each minute to pass by so I could lend aid to plotting the overthrow of this oppressive government. I'd much rather be doing that than serving them. The silence in Tipedre was deafening. The past two weeks made the city appear to be bipolar in a sense, loud and bustling during the day but lifeless and vacant at night. Nothing but the sound of a few soldiers having their conversations and patriotic citizens who defied the curfew and were being apprehended by law enforcement lent any sound to the quiet night. Oh, how I longed for the day when I march into the presidential palace to throw DeOrtiz out onto the street. That is the day I will feel like a real soldier. The day I will fulfill my duty in protecting San Diamo from all its threats by deposing the one that lied within her borders.

"Santano!" a voice cried. "Come over here."

I turned around and saw Captain Vasquez and a group of other soldiers sitting at a table outside a bar. Vasquez and the other men were all a part of my nightly patrol unit that watched over the southern perimeter of the presidential mansion. Yes, protecting the home of the felon that lives inside it and ensuring that he slept well at night. If only he knew that his nights inside that mansion were numbered. Regardless, there was nothing else interesting that was happening at that moment, and I decided to entertain myself with some light conversation.

"You've been working too hard," said Vasquez. "Sit and join us,"

They were playing a game of cards. It was Spades. I enjoyed this game, so why not lighten the mood. I sat down and prepared to play as Vasquez placed a cigar in between his teeth, greeting me with a brash grin.

"Best of luck to you Juan," chuckled Private Roberto. "The captain has yet to lose a game."

"No need for luck Roberto. I'm skilled in this game. As a matter of fact, they called me Spades where I'm from,"

The captain laughed as he shuffled the cards, "Apparently you haven't heard the saying, 'glass, china, and reputation are easily cracked, and never mended well.' Let's see if that name has any weight."

A few minutes had passed, and the captain now had sweat running down his face while I was calmly preparing to add yet another victory to my impeccable record.

"Maybe that name does have weight to it, Spade," he said as he dropped his cards on the table in defeat.

I laughed, "looks like my reputation won't be cracked tonight captain,"

Both I, the captain, and the rest of the soldiers all laughed together. I thought to myself that this was perhaps the most enjoyable night that I have had in such a long while. The captain laid back in his chair and lit his cigar.

"It's alright, my big victory will be coming soon," said Vasquez.

"What do you mean?" asked Roberto

"When I finally get to the top, that is where all the money is. Once I rise in the ranks, I'll have so much money that most of it would just seem useless to me. I'll be just like the other bastards running the army these days."

I was enraged. "So, you're fine with being just like them!? Those crooks who work for DeOrtiz!?"

The captain appeared to be upset by my outburst but carried on smoking his cigar as if I said nothing.

"Yes, I agree that DeOrtiz and the higher-ups are corrupt," Vasquez replied nonchalantly. "But they sit at the top and the top there is wealth. Wealth is what is needed to survive in this world Santano and I want to be where the wealth is,"

The blood in my veins began to boil. I was sitting across a morally bankrupt man who, unfortunately, was my superior. It took a monumental amount of restraint for me to not use any form of violence against the captain at that moment. Luckily for him, the attention of our patrol unit was suddenly taken away by a shadowy masked figure wearing a hood lurking past us.

"Stop right there!" yelled Vasquez.

The masked figure began to run towards the southern end of the city. My patrol members immediately picked up our weapons and gave chase to the suspicious person. We ran through a market, through narrow alleyways, and even on rooftops. We continued to shout our demands for the swift, masked person to stop. A few of us fired a few shots hoping to slow him/her down but the incredibly athletic bandit simply ignored and evaded our every attempt. During our chase, we followed the hooded individual to a courtyard in a small community, but we lost sight of where he/she went. The roads in the community were narrow with little to no passable space between the houses and there were dead ends at almost every turn. Whoever this strange person was, they ran directly into an intricate maze.

"Fan out!" Vasquez ordered.

Each of us promptly separated into different directions. There I was slowly and stealthily walking through the narrow corridors with my rifle out in front of me, ready to attack at a moment's notice and cautiously surveying every corner as I go along. I eventually stopped after hearing a panting sound coming from behind me. I slowly turned around and made my way toward the sounds that seemed to be coming from underneath an old, covered table. As I approached the table, I was suddenly surprised by a rock that was thrown at me from underneath it. I managed to dodge the projectile and the hooded person emerged from underneath the table, flipping it onto it's side in the process. I alone gave chance and pursued the individual to a high-walled dead end.

"Stop!" I shouted.

With nowhere left to go, the person their hands in surrender and removed the hood that covered their head revealing long, flowing hair blowing in the wind. It was a woman. I slowly approached the individual, ready to apprehend her. However, she would not be taken so easily. She immediately turned around and attacked me. I could tell she was a skilled fighter as she effortlessly disarmed me of my weapon. The two of us were now engaged in hand-to-hand combat. I managed to remove her mask during the scuffle and tackled her to the ground.

As I had her within my firm grip, I looked at her face. She was young, apparently no more than nineteen years old. I then glanced at her forearm and was shocked by what I saw. She had the viper head tattoo as well. She was a sister of mine within the resistance. During my lack of concentration, the mysterious young girl was able to break free from my grasp and brandish a knife which she then used to cut my right forearm before leaping onto the high wall, then onto the rooftops to make her escape. She was more tigress than viper.

I remained sitting on the ground with my back against a wall, exhausted and nursing my wound. The knife had cut across the viper tattoo I had just received a few weeks ago. The symbol of a just cause, now tarnished. I cut off a piece of my sleeve so I could tie it around the wound to stop the bleeding.

"Santano!" I heard a voice cry.

I looked up the corridor to see Vasquez and the rest of the squad running toward me.

"Where did the runner go?" he asked me.

"She escaped," I replied as I rose to my feet.

"Very well then, let's head back to our post,"

I looked at my watch and I noticed it was 8:40 PM, the meeting was going to start in twenty minutes. Seeing as I was already in the southern end of the city and the warehouse wasn't farther from where I was, I decided to try to leave my squad to make my way there.

"Captain," I said fatigued. "I'm injured. Could I go home to rest for the night?"

The captain inspected my wound and then denied my request, saying that the injury was "minor". I knew that it was a minor, however, my duties required me to be somewhere else; and deserting your squad was a punishable offense within the army. However, I was still determined to try.

"Captain, I'm sore and bruised from fighting the runner, may I please return home to nurse my wounds."

"Do as you wish Santano!" he said rather annoyed.

Captain Vasquez and the rest of my squadron made their return to their post. I was now free of my duties and proceeded to hastily make my way to the warehouse. I had arrived just two minutes before the meeting had begun and showed my now slashed tattoo at the entrance of the warehouse. When I entered, I noticed that the room was not full of those adoring Caesar believers as before. It was simply Caesar, Hector, and a few other unfamiliar faces all sitting at the makeshift bar engaging in a discussion. I made my way over to them; they were all gathered around a map of Tipedre that was sitting on the bar counter.

"Juan! I'm glad you could make it," said Caesar. "You look beat up, is everything alright?"

"I'm fine," I answered. "I had a little incident on my way here,"

The doors of the warehouse opened once more and the young girl that had cut me entered the room.

"Sorry for being late," she said while trying to catch her breath.

She then glanced at me, "what is he doing here!?" she snapped. "He's working with the soldiers. They chased me on my way here!"

"So, you two have met I see," replied Caesar.

"I can bet she was the one that cut your arm," Hector interjected sarcastically

The young girl gazed upon me with fury and mistrust in her eyes as if she was ready to cut more than just more forearm. To pacify the situation, Caesar stepped in.

"Juan, this is Mesilinda Encarto. She is a member of our group. Her father was a detective who was investigating a money laundering scheme that involved one of DeOrtiz's close business allies, but he was wrongfully arrested and charged before he could complete his work. She hasn't seen him since then,"

"I'm sorry to hear that," I said softly as I looked at Mesilinda.

She simply ignored me. "What are we discussing?" she asked Caesar.

"Now that we're all gathered, I called you all here tonight to discuss the plans to proceed with our revolution," Caesar said firmly. "I have already been in contact with the rest of our leaders in other cities. We plan to strike on the final night of curfew which is three nights from now when DeOrtiz and all his allies should least expect anything."

I looked around the circle while Caesar was speaking to take note of the men that would be playing a part in our revolutionary plans. In the circle was Raul Borgias, a wealthy bank owner whose gut was as big as his pockets. He once was close friends with DeOrtiz but was no longer associated with him due to bad business, Geraldo Santiago, a prominent leader in the opposition party, a bald British journalist by the name of Roger Ambrose who owned a small newspaper outlet in Tipedre, a quiet, middle-aged judge named Claudia Paulo, Eduardo Luciano, Tipedre's Chief of Police, Hector, and Mesilinda. I was unclear as to what purpose each of us would serve in Caesar's plans. It was quite the assortment of individuals, however, I kept telling myself that so long as DeOrtiz was removed from power all would be fine.

"Many of our members serve in the military, the police force, and are average members of the public," Caesar said. "If we are to be successful, we are to use the tomorrow to spread the word to other people within the public so that they can join and give us strength in numbers."

"I can help spread the word across the city," Mesilinda suggested. "I know many university students who will be happy to join us,"

"I can also have my company print out a few papers tomorrow announcing the revolution," said Ambrose. "I will do my best to ensure that they are solely distributed to people who will be loyal to our cause in the civilian areas both in and around the city."

Caesar agreed with these suggestions and ordered that I help circulate the news of the revolution to the public. Caesar then, along with the help of Hector used the map to then layout an intricate plan for where they would station tanks, troops, and some loyal police members within the city as they march on and lay siege to the presidential mansion, mayor's office the High Court, and the congressional building.

Tipedre was a coastal city and the largest in San Diamo. It is famous for its beaches, hotels, markets, businesses, colonial architecture, shipping docks, and ports. It was a major transit hub that was fitted with a web of several highways and railways that led to and from the city. There was also a major airport that lay at the eastern end of the city. Caesar suggested cutting off access to the docks, ports, and airport as well as blocking all major roads would be vital to our plans. In addition to this, many residential areas are laid on the outskirts of the city, so citizens have an easy commute. In the heart of Tipedre is where you can find the presidential mansion and the congressional building and if you go in the direction of downtown Tipedre, you can find the mayor's office and the High Court. All major roads lead to these buildings and the plan was to encircle and capture them. The nearest military base is seven miles northwest of the city, just across the Rio Grande River. That was also where all DeOrtiz's military friends resided. Taking the base to limit any outside support from DeOrtiz loyalists and isolate the city would work to our advantage by limiting any fighting. Caesar displayed his strategic and tactical brilliance. Once again, Caesar showed proof of his reputation.

Taking Tipedre, and other major cities such as San Miguel in the north, and Lobrano in the south would ensure our victory. The goal at the end of this operation would be to install Mr. Santiago as the next president. I was not a fan of politicians, but, if Mr. Santiago was an ally in our fight, I suppose he would be a suitable leader for San Diamo. We discussed the plan for hours, carefully and calculatingly fine-tuning every detail. It was all coming together perfectly. Everyone at the table understood their roles perfectly. However, I had one slight concern.

"Will there be fighting?" I asked. "Will people have to die?"

The room became silent as all eyes turned toward Caesar.

"I do not want any fighting to occur," he reassured. "If there is any bloodshed then there will also be a high chance of civil war. I cannot promise you that it will not come to that, but my intention is for this to be a speedy and well-executed military overthrow that is supported by the people. And I believe with the support we have, that is possible,"

His words didn't do much to ease my concerns, but I suppose that I would have to trust him. San Diamo's salvation was now just three nights away. It was now in our hands and my heart was beaming with optimism and excitement for the future that was about to be ushered into existence. In just three short nights the winds of change will blow over this once proud nation. At long last, a new era had arrived.

5

THE VIPER'S BITE

THE THREE DAYS HAD NOW passed. It was April 23, 1984, the date that will forever be etched in history as the day San Diamo was restored to her former glory. The day of the revolution. The sun seemed to burn in the sky with greater radiance and a stinging chill cut across the entire country as the wind passed through. There was a nerve-racking intensity in the atmosphere that only grew with every passing minute. Goosebumps plagued my body, and my stomach was in knots. The only days in my life that I could recall feeling similar to this were my wedding day or the days when my children were born. Except, the wedding aisle will be the roads of the capital and a new nation would be birthed.

I was incredibly restless during the night. Eliza tried to console me but to no avail, my mind was consumed with anxiety, and I was unable to sleep for more than an hour or two. I had spent the past two days doing what Caesar had asked of me, notifying people in the city of the revolution, and convincing them to join. Within just twenty-four hours, talks of the revolution spread across Tipedre like wildfire. It was on the tongues of market vendors and customers and made for conversations in the bars and barbershops. It was discussed between neighbors and talked about at dinner tables. Mr. Ambrose and his newspaper company did a remarkable job at producing papers that promoted the revolution while keeping it away from the hands of DeOrtiz loyalists. The national media was completely oblivious to what was brewing in the country, it was the most well-kept and well-organized secret in San Diamo for the past two days. But soon enough, the news of DeOrtiz's downfall will make the headlines. Life was seemingly normal in San Diamo for the past forty-eight hours, but that was also what the leaders of Troy believed before their eventual fall.

I woke up at the break of dawn and went into the bathroom to wash my face. As I stared at my reflection in the mirror and observed my now scarred viper tattoo, I reflected on how rapidly my life had changed in just the span of a short fortnight. I was never much of a believer in fate and destiny, but the past two weeks served only to challenge my beliefs. How did a poor, simple farmer who left his hometown in search of a better life find himself involved in plotting a revolution? Many great men of history came from humble beginnings, but I was no great man, just simply a man that cares only for his family and his country. Life is an unpredictable and strange thing I thought to myself, but if this is my ordained purpose; then I will commit myself to see it through.

I could not risk having Eliza and my children stay in the city to-night. I told my wife that the military received intelligence of a possible violent riot occurring in the city and that the army was tasked to stay in the city and stand guard. Therefore, for her safety and that of our chil-dren, I suggested that they spend the night in Capacha, our hometown, with her parents. Of course, I still couldn't reveal to her my involvement with Viper and of course, there was no way for me to know if tonight's events would become violent. I had to guarantee my family's safety so it would be best for them to be as far away from the city as possible. I helped Eliza pack, woke our children, drove them to the train station, and bided them farewell. I would return for them once I knew that it was safe enough for them to come home.

The intensity in the air grew as the hours ticked by. The revolution was scheduled to begin at 6 PM when most of the city's residents were beginning to go home in time for the curfew. It was currently 5 PM, I was at home alone and getting dressed in my uniform to make my way into the city. The sky was blanketed by thick dark clouds and the wind was blasting through the trees. Everyone in the city seemed to look either anxious or ready to unleash their fury on DeOrtiz and avenge what had happened in the capital just two weeks ago. As I walked through the city, I ran into Mesilinda wearing her iconic black hood on the corner of the main street which led directly to the presidential mansion.

"Are you ready?" I asked as I walked up behind her.

She didn't look at me, instead, her eyes were fixed on the large pearly white building with the enormous gate that stood up the street before us.

"That monster took my father away," she said tearfully. "After today, I'll see him again."

"We must get to our positions," she added. We both then left the street corner and in just a few minutes, the revolution will begin.

It was 5:45 PM and the night was beginning to set in. Thunder began to rumble through the sky as the rain began to sprinkle down on San Diamo. I arrived at my assigned position just three city blocks away from the congressional building. As the minutes slowly ticked by, I grew ever more anxious. My heart could not stop galloping in my chest. No matter what, tonight had to be executed perfectly, or else the consequences would be dire. A few soldiers were beginning to fill the streets for the final night of curfew, Caesar said many of them were a part of Viper, and as I looked around, I couldn't help but wonder who among them were allies and who were the enemies. I went to sit in an alleyway with my rifle by my side to try to calm my nerves before the revolution began. Suddenly, I felt the ground beginning to rumble, and loud sounds of shouting and footsteps coming from every possible direction.

I looked up the street and to my amazement, I saw the army marching through with the might of tanks and other armored vehicles behind them. It was as if they were marching towards war. But it wasn't just the power of the army that proceeded up the road to the congressional building, the soldiers were accompanied by the sheer might of the Diaman people behind them. Hundreds upon thousands of people; young and old, students and workers, men, women, and even some young children all swarmed the streets of Tipedre in defiance. DeOrtiz's judgment had now arrived at long last, and I intended to give my full participation.

The rain began to pour down like showers of blessings from the Lord. I pushed my way through the thick crowds so that I could be amongst the other foot soldiers, but I was unable to get close to them. I was, however, able to get close enough to one of the tanks and gain a firm grip on it which I then used to climb on top of it. While on the tank en route to congress I looked out across Tipedre and was awe-struck by the incalculable number of people that I saw protesting in the rain to demand that DeOrtiz steps down at once. I had only seen this night within the figment of my imagination, but I would have never believed that it would have come to reality. Tears filled my eyes as I was overwhelmed with emotions. The people were united, the army was at their side, and due to that, victory was in our grasp.

When my unit arrived at the congressional building, soldiers began to disperse and encircle its perimeter. The people cheered us on with great enthusiasm. It was a far different feeling than what was experienced just two weeks ago when the army had brawled with them, but we were able to put aside our differences and show them that we are not the pawns that they thought we were. As the tanks approached the gates of congress, the crowds chanted "¡toma el edificio!" (Take the building!). Without further delay, the tanks plowed through the gates of congress as the soldiers and a few citizens followed suit into the yard of the massive castle-like building to seize it. A few soldiers even stormed into the building to secure the inside. I looked out from on top of the tank and saw a camera crew in the yard capturing this moment of history. The eyes of the nation were on Tipedre. This was a day that was second only to our Independence Day some might even consider this rainy night as our second independence.

As I dismounted from the tank, I along with a few other soldiers stood guard outside the congress doors to ensure that none of the citizens entered the building. I could hear screams and soldiers shouting commands to those who were inside the building that night. They were searching for members of DeOrtiz's party who enabled his corruption and apprehending them. Cleansing the halls of congress of its scum, something that was well needed. After a few minutes, a soldier who had stormed inside the building ran back out and announced at the top of his lungs "we've secured the mansion! The city is ours!". The crowd immediately erupted into cheers. I was overjoyed but I also could not believe it. Caesar's plan worked to absolute perfection and not a single shot was fired, nor a life lost. It took us only two short hours to secure the city. The speed and proficiency at which the plan was executed left me in awe.

The crowds began to celebrate with songs and dance in the wet streets. However, the real celebration was at the presidential mansion. When I was done reflecting on our swift victory, I ran out of the congress yard to make my way to the mansion. While on my way there, I observed the looks of happiness and jubilation that was on the faces of the people that night. I have not seen such a celebration in such a long time. This victory, this night, belonged to the people and I carried a sense of pride knowing that I had helped to deliver it. The rain had washed away the old San Diamo and had now helped the new one bloom.

I arrived at the presidential mansion to see hundreds of people outside its walls celebrating, more journalists reporting the momentous occasion, its gates already trampled by tanks and armored vehicles, and soldiers surrounding its perimeter. Maneuvering my way through the crowds was almost impossible. There was very little to no space to walk, it was amazing that people were able to breathe.

"People of San Diamo!" a voice cried over a microphone.

I looked toward the steps of the mansion, and my eyes were captured in shock by what I saw. Caesar himself held tightly to a handcuffed DeOrtiz and held a microphone to his mouth. He appeared to be visibly shaken by what was happening. How fitting was this, we had lived like prisoners under DeOrtiz for so long, and now, he was ours. A dead silence fell over the area surrounding the mansion, and DeOrtiz spoke.

"Given the events of tonight, the will of the people has been made clear. All heads of the military and some elected officials have been apprehended. I am ordering those members of the army that are loyal to the elected government, to stand down immediately and not engage in any confrontation. Also, effective immediately; I Fredicio DeOrtiz will abdicate my duties as President of San Diamo,"

A thunderous roar of celebration that echoed throughout the nation's borders was released into the rainy night sky. DeOrtiz was promptly taken away by soldiers and I fell to my knees as tears of joy began to run down my face. What had been accomplished tonight was something that I had no words to describe. DeOrtiz 's reign was over. A new hope had been ignited within the hearts of all who were there that night. The people of San Diamo will rest tonight knowing that they will awake in a new nation, one that had been reborn. This night only proved that real power rested with those who give it, not those who wield it. This night proved that vipers were stronger than even lions.

6

EL LIBERTADOR

IN THE CHRISTIAN FAITH, THERE is a well-known story that I was always told when I boy going to church, of Noah and his ark. This age-old tale says that God was greatly displeased with mankind due to their sins and because of this, he sent rain for forty days and forty nights. It rained so heavily during this time, that the earthly water bodies began to overflow, and caused a great flood that wiped out most of human and beast kind. However, God spared Noah and his family due to their righteousness and ordered Noah to construct a massive ark so that he and his family may live and repopulate the earth. Of course, during last night's showers, God thankfully didn't flood the earth but like what he did back then during the great flood, San Diamo's greatest sin was wiped away once and for all. Poetic justice, what a lovely thing it is.

The next morning had come, and the rain had ceased. There was a tranquility that was flowing in the air and the disdain that the people had for DeOrtiz's leadership was made more evident by the looks of sheer joy and happiness that were on their faces now that it was over. It felt as if a tremendous burden was lifted off the shoulders of the country and chains were removed from the throats of its people so that they could now breathe. What a remarkable feeling it was.

Two days after the revolution, Eliza and my children returned home to Tipedre. I warmly embraced them at the train station as if I was just returning from a long and grueling war. I had finally found the courage to tell Eliza of my involvement in Viper and how I helped in orchestrating the revolution. I had thought that she would've immediately berated me for lying to her, instead she looked at me with tears in her eyes and gave me a glowing proud smile. She then kissed me on the cheek and gazed into my eyes with a look of love and adoration as she called me a 'hero'. And for the first time in my life, I felt like I was.

It would be a crime if such an astounding victory was to go uncelebrated. As San Diamo culture would demand, massive festivals and parades must be held. That was the law of the land for momentous occasions such as this, and the law-abiding citizens of San Diamo obliged. On the same day, when my family and I were reunited, Tipedre came alive in a grand jubilee. Such euphoria had gone dormant under DeOrtiz's time in office. The city's atmosphere overflowed with the melodies of vibrant music and the aroma of a wide array of delectable foods. The people danced to their heart's content as confetti in the national colors of blue, white, and gold rained down from off the rooftops. It was as if the Carnaval came early this year and all of Tipedre's four million residents were in attendance. What made this experience better was that I was able to spend it with my family, the people I risked everything with my involvement with Viper for. To see my children Maria, and Julio play with other young children in an improved San Diamo that would now offer hope to them brought tears to my eyes. What a rewarding feeling. What a time to be alive.

The main event of that glorious day was still to come in the afternoon. The victory parade was yet to come and the road to the presidential mansion, the sight of our triumph, would be the final lap of the procession. I quickly gathered Eliza and the children, and we made our way to Capital Road, the street leading to the mansion, to prepare. The audience came out in droves as they lined the sides of the sidewalks preparing to see their heroes go by. I was truly stunned by how much the mood in Tipedre had changed in just two short weeks, nonetheless, the collective delight that reverberated around the city was welcomed. We waited with great anticipation for the procession to pass. Poor Maria was beginning to become restless as she tugged at my leg and continuously badgered me with the question "when will they come papa?". I picked her up and put her on my shoulders then suddenly the echo of loud cheering began to inch closer in our direction.

As the cheering and the music began to crescendo, we could see the procession of tanks, armored vehicles, and marching bands emerging in the distance. The people raved in celebration as the parade passed by. The pride I felt was indescribable. There was one part of the parade, however, which caught my eye. Riding on a donkey in the middle of the procession like a humble king on the way to his coronation was Caesar, fitted in his army uniform and his iconic shaded glasses as he waved and gave a few salutes to the people as he made his way up to the presidential mansion. I found it strange yet, gratifying that Caesar would make himself a part of the parade. After all, he was the mastermind behind toppling DeOrtiz, perhaps the people should know who lead the struggle for their liberation. Maybe they should be introduced to their champion on the back of a steed who held a handcuffed DeOrtiz on the steps of the presidential mansion in the rain as he abdicated. Caesar was the real hero, and a hero must be treated as such.

The tanks and armored vehicles that were at the front of the procession pulled over to the sidewalks in front of the mansion thus allowing Caesar to enter through its dented gates to make his way up to the steps where a podium and a microphone waited for him at the top. This scene was familiar to me. Caesar was going to give one of his fiery speeches like he did that night in the warehouse. Caesar was not just a military genius, he was also a spectacular orator, and who best ignite a sense of optimism into the hearts of the people than him? Mr. Santiago must've planned for Caesar to speak today, though I found it odd that I did not see him during the parade. How strange.

As Caesar dismounted his horse and made his way up the steps of the mansion to the podium, the crowd began to gather to get a closer look at him and to hear him speak. The anticipation from the audience was equal, if not, similar to what was felt that night in the warehouse. Everyone's eyes and ears were focused on Caesar, he had their undivided attention. Caesar stood at the podium with a strong and imposing demeanor as two soldiers, whom I assume were Viper agents, stood behind him for his protection. Caesar removed his glasses, raised his hands to silence the crowd, then finally, he spoke.

"People of San Diamo!" he shouted. "This is your day!"

He continued by saying, "allow me to introduce myself. My name is Lieutenant Louis Caesar. For seven long years, you have unfairly endured the weight of tyranny and injustice on your shoulders. But you did not break nor yield, instead, your will held strong, and now; you are free!"

A thunderous round of cheering and applause arose from the audience as Caesar gave his speech. The charisma and passion he spoke with brought a feeling of nostalgia as I recalled how moved I was that night in the warehouse. Caesar spoke a galvanizing message of change and hope. A message about creating equal opportunities for San Diamo's poor and forgotten by challenging the wealthy elite and holding those in power accountable. A message that inspired optimism for future generations of Diaman people. The audience loved and supported every word that came from Caesar's mouth. His aura of contagious inspiration infected everyone in his presence. The people came together in unison and chanted "el libertador! El libertador! El libertador!" ("the liberator!"), that was the new name that was bestowed on Caesar.

Once again, I was overwhelmed by the feeling of hope that washed over me, and I did not doubt that it filled the hearts of all those in attendance. At that moment of encapsulation, Caesar quickly became the most venerated and revered individual in San Diamo. Caesar concluded his speech and descended the steps of the mansion into a swarm of people who were desperate to shake the hand of their savior, or at the very least, touch him as we walked by. His two soldiers tried to push the crowd back, but the people were relentless. Caesar was San Diamo's newest celebrity, and his adoring fans would stop at nothing to be close to him.

During the ruckus, however, Caesar saw me as I was preparing to leave with my family.

"Juan!" he called out to me.

I sent Eliza and the children on their way before leaving to speak with him.

"That was an excellent speech Caesar," I said. "you've become quite the hero."

"We are all heroes. We were the ones who created this day. I could've never done this alone," he said as he pulled me over to a corner of the mansion's yard for us to speak in private.

"Is that your family over there?" he then asked. "They're beautiful. I'm happy to know that they'll be living in a much better country soon, one that you helped to fight for,"

"It's a great feeling indeed," I replied as I looked at Eliza and my children.

"Where was Mr. Santiago?" I then asked.

Caesar paused for a second and looked deep into my eyes.

"Mr. Santiago was not feeling well, so he sent me to give a speech on his behalf. Actually, that is what I needed to talk with you about. Can you dress nicely and be here again tomorrow afternoon? I need you for something important,"

"Yes, I can be here," I said without giving it much thought.

"Excellent! Gracias Juan. I'll see you here tomorrow," he said to me before mounting his donkey and leaving the premises.

I had no clue of what Caesar wanted me to do tomorrow, nor did I ask. I trusted his judgment and felt quite honored that he would choose me to join him in what he had planned. I stood and watched as Caesar trotted away with a caravan of people following behind him. In all honesty, I would much prefer if Caesar was the one to take the mantle of the next president rather than another lying career politician. He was more suited for that role in my opinion. However, if Caesar believed that Mr. Santiago was to assume that role in his stead, I will not question it. So long as Caesar was to play an influential role in shaping the country's future, then that would be something both I and perhaps, all of San Diamo would support. Wouldn't that be a better path forward?

7

THE BODYGUARD

I WOKE UP THE FOLLOWING day to another brilliant and unusually scorching hot spring morning. It was a special day in my family as it was my son Julio's twelfth birthday. I was the last to wake up that morning. Pondering on what Caesar had planned for me today left me restless throughout most of the night. I was also contemplating how to tell Julio that I wouldn't spend the day with him as I normally do on this occasion. Nevertheless, my son was getting older and sooner or later he would have to understand that a man must attend to his duties. I entered the kitchen to see Eliza and the children already having a chat around the table. I gazed at my son for a while, admiring how much he had grown and imagining the bright future that he and his sister would now get to enjoy. That is perhaps the best present that he could receive today.

"Happy birthday my son," I said as I greeted him with a hug at the table.

I then presented Julio with his gift. I gave him a small rectangular box in blue gift wrap with a gold-colored ribbon tied around it. Julio took quickly snatched the box from my hands with a wide and bright little boy's grin on his face. Julio wasted no time in ripping the gift wrap off and opening the box to find a pocketknife inside with the words "blood and duty" carved into its handle. I gave it to him as a symbol of his now fast-approaching manhood.

"You can't give a boy a knife for his birthday!" Eliza lashed out at me.

"He'll be a man soon, it will come in handy for him one day," I tried to reassure her.

She then proceeded to take the knife from Julio and put it back in its box.

"I'll get you something nicer later ok," she said to Julio as she rubbed his head with motherly compassion before leaving the room.

"I liked the gift papa," Julio said. "But I guess I'll have to wait till I'm older to use it."

I smiled at my son and knelt before him to give him some fatherly advice.

"Blood and duty son. A man must always stand up for what he knows in his heart is right and must commit himself to doing what is always right. Always remember that."

"Shouldn't you be preparing to go somewhere now?" Eliza reminded me.

I had almost forgotten about my meeting with Caesar. I quickly prepared something to eat, dressed in my best casual attire, wished my family well, and then finally made my way to the presidential mansion. Life in Tipedre was returning to normalcy now that the revolution had passed, and the new sense of hope that sat on the faces of its residents was unignorable. I arrived at the mansion on time, exited my car, and then proceeded to make my way into the mansion's yard. I entered the premises to see Caesar, uncharacteristically dressed in a formal grey business-like suit with a white shirt and navy-blue tie, standing next to a jet-black vehicle with another man who was dressed in a chauffer's uniform.

"Juan! I'm so glad you could make it," Caesar said as he greeted me. "You look good,"

"Gracias. So do you, my friend," I answered as I firmly shook his hands.

The driver then opened the passenger door of the vehicle that was next to where Caesar and I were standing.

"Shall we?" Caesar asked with a gentleman's charm.

I, along with Caesar, then entered the rear passenger side of the vehicle, and we sped off into the city shortly afterward.

"May I ask where we are going?" I queried.

"We're going to congress. There's an important speech I need to give," Caesar replied.

Ah, yes. Another one of Caesar's famous speeches. Congress had now resumed its proceedings and now they were tasked with constructing a better nation in the aftermath of the revolution and DeOrtiz's overthrow from office. Congress now knew that if they failed in their obligations, the people would hold them accountable, and who better to solidify that message than the man who united the people to bring down the nation's former failed leader? Caesar sat in the car relaxed and displaying little to no emotion at all. Just completely unnerved by the thought of giving a speech of this magnitude. I had no clue of what words Caesar was skillfully jotting down in his mind, the only thing I was certain of was that once he began orating, those words would resound with all those who hear them.

"Will Mr. Santiago be in attendance?" I asked.

"I'm not so sure," he answered. "We'll find out once we get there."

"Juan," he then said as he turned to me "There is an offer I would like to make you. I am about to take on a more important role in the affairs of the country and for this role, I need people I can trust. My protection will be of the utmost importance in the near future. Therefore, I am offering you the position to serve as my bodyguard,"

I immediately froze in shock and was rather dumbfounded by Caesar's offer. He was a far more skilled soldier than I, and was fully capable of protecting himself, why would Caesar need me for his protection? He was also beloved in both the military and the public, who would dare try to harm him? I looked into Caesar's eyes and saw just how serious he was with his offer.

"What about Hector?" I asked him. "Isn't he better for this?"

"Yes, I did consider Hector. But I will need him for a much different task. So do you accept my offer or not?"

I was still awfully confused by Caesar's request, but after a few minutes of thought, I accepted his offer.

There was another issue on my mind that I wanted to be clarified. Just how exactly was Caesar able to easily carry out his revolution plan? Just how exactly was he able to rally so many people, both the powerful and otherwise, to his cause? The question laid heavy on my mind for some time now, and now was the best time to get my answer.

"Caesar, it's been on my mind for a while now. How were you able to get so many people to join Viper and support the revolution? How were you able to know who would be loyal and who would be traitors?"

Caesar's eyes were fixed on staring out the window as the car drove by.

"The revolution was the result of years' worth of planning and preparation," he explained. "Not all of those people that night were members of Viper, but Viper was responsible for setting the revolution in motion, and the people are the greatest weapon you can have in any revolution,"

He went on by saying, "people have expectations Juan, and when those expectations aren't met, they turn into grievances, and people will follow those who are willing to resolve those grievances. Think of it as a marriage. The wife and the husband both have expectations of one another, but if those expectations are consistently not met, or if there is no effort in trying at the very least; then even the most loyal and loving husband or wife will turn against their significant other,"

Caesar's eloquent response painted a vivid picture in my head. He never ceases to amaze me whenever he speaks. As our conversation ended, the vehicle entered the yard of the congressional building, its gates still dented pieces of metal on the ground. News crews from across the country flocked toward us to capture San Diamo's newest celebrity as he entered the halls of congress. My first task as Caesar's new bodyguard was to navigate a path through the sea of Journalists so that he could walk freely while they bombarded him with questions. Afterward, we entered the building, its halls of marble flooring, historical artifacts, and luxurious décor that was ransacked just a few days ago now fully restored to its former glory.

Caesar walked through the halls of congress with a swagger that highlighted the confident mindset he had as he prepared to give his speech to congress. At the end of the hall, just across the building's rotunda, was congress's chamber. When Caesar and I approached the chamber doors the two guards standing by promptly opened them to welcome us as if they knew of our visit. When we entered the room, all 305 of the remaining lawmakers who were not arrested the night of the revolution immediately silenced their heated debates as their eyes were now locked on Caesar. That was 145 lawmakers fewer than usual. I was astonished by how his mere presence was able to silence a room of some of the most powerful men and women in the country in a matter of seconds. Caesar garnered quite the reputation for how he brought DeOrtiz to justice that night on the steps of the presidential mansion. They knew of Caesar, and they knew he was their reckoner.

I walked closely behind Caesar as he made his way through the aisle up to the speaker's podium. That podium was only used by the head of the congress, the vice-president, or the president if he were to give a speech, but now; Caesar commanded it. I took a seat in the front row next to the aisle and sat quietly as Caesar prepared himself. New crews filled the chamber, which meant that the eyes of the nation were on Caesar and its ears will be listening closely to what he had to say. There was no doubt that tomorrow's headlines would be whatever it is that Caesar would have to say.

However, there was something strange that caught my eye. Mr. Santiago was not in attendance. Why would the next president not be in attendance for something such as this? Doesn't he know that his consistent absence would be a major blight on his first impression on the nation? Perhaps he was still ill, and he had asked Caesar to give another speech for him. I would advise him to be careful though. If he does not get well soon and starts taking on his new role, people might think that Caesar is the new president of San Diamo. And who could blame them if they did?

The room stood still, and all eyes were fixed on Caesar. He stood at the podium with his usual strong and poised demeanor, cleared his throat, took a deep breath; then finally he let his voice be heard.

"Ladies and gentlemen of the congress, good afternoon and thank you for having me," he greeted the room.

"For those of you who do not know me, my name is Louis Caesar. I am a former lieutenant of the army, and I am also the man who plotted the revolution that ended the former president's tenure. I will be brief, for my main purpose of being here today, is to simply tell every single one of you in this room that you have all failed,"

He went on to say, "when the people of San Diamo needed you the most you sat idly by as the former president drove the nation and its people into destitution. It is reprehensible and quite frankly, unforgivable as well. However, the focus should now be on building a better nation, one that works for all its people and that will therefore require that we put aside our differences, foster unity, and comradery, and commit to achieving this common goal. Order must be restored, accountability must be taken, and the trust of the people must be earned. I have pondered the best path forward for some time now, and it has become clear to me what must be done to assure our mutual success,"

The air in the room grew so thick with each passing minute of his speech that breathing became daunting. I have heard Caesar give striking speeches before, but none like this. Some of the lawmakers looked at him with anger in their eyes, some appeared to be intimidated while others did their best to conceal their emotions. One thing was certain, however, the next set of words that leave Caesar's lips would indeed send shockwaves across San Diamo. Caesar took a deep breath, then made his announcement.

"What is needed in our nation right now is strong leadership that is for the people. Therefore, I announce that for the next three years, I Louis Gabriel Caesar will serve as the next president of San Diamo,"

Within that same second, the entire room immediately erupted into a mad frenzy. Almost every lawmaker began to heckle and voice their disapproval of Caesar's sudden claim to power. I, on the other hand, sat in complete shock and disbelief over what I had just heard. I was conflicted. On one hand, I was elated that Caesar would serve as the next president and I supported him, yet, on the other hand; I was confused and somewhat appalled by this decision. What could've possibly been Caesar's motivation for shattering the initial plan of passing power to Mr. Santiago? And, most importantly, what would this mean for San Diamo?

As the jeering and the vocal disagreements continued, the doors of the chamber suddenly flew open. Several soldiers suddenly marched in with weapons drawn, pointing them at the lawmakers and ordering them to "get down". In that dramatic moment, the heckling immediately came to a halt as the congressmen and women all cowered on the floor. During all this, Caesar stood at the podium completely unnerved. It was clear that this was his doing. He had just put one of the most powerful bodies in all the land under submission.

"Will there be any further objections?" Caesar asked sarcastically.

Not a single lawmaker responded. At that moment, Caesar acquired all power in San Diamo and placed it on full display for the entire nation to see. As for me, I was no longer tasked with guarding the life of my friend and a man that I respect highly, I was now tasked with protecting the president of San Diamo. Caesar's actions led me to question him more than I ever did before, but my heart wants to believe that he will be a phenomenal leader. I suppose the next three years will give me the answers to my burning question. What kind of leader will Caesar be?

8

VENOM

SIX MONTHS HAVE NOW PASSED since Caesar seized the presidency. One would think that taking control of the nation's highest office in the way he did would be a major cause for concern that would've lost him the support of the public, but ironically, it didn't. The public loved what Caesar did that day in the congress. In their eyes, Caesar was right. All the politicians in congress did fail them during the DeOrtiz's administration and Caesar's actions were justified for it was his way of holding them accountable and letting them know that from that day forward, they served the people. Almost overnight, Caesar became a symbol of hope. Never mind his rather violent and undemocratic methods, Caesar was the light that destroyed the darkness of corrupt power and so long as he was fighting on behalf of the people then he had their support. Caesar did say that the people were his greatest weapon after all.

Caesar was inaugurated one week after his infamous speech to congress on the steps of the presidential mansion in front of a massive crowd of people who flocked to the capital city to see their hero take the oath of office. There were so many people in Tipedre that day that traffic coming into the city was stalled so badly that it even extended to nearby towns outside of the city. They welcomed their new president by chanting his new moniker 'el libertador' so loudly that even neighboring countries must've heard it. Caesar represented hope and change to the people. He was unlike anything they had seen before. He wasn't just another member of the establishment, he was simply a man on a mission to help his people, and for that; he enjoyed the privilege of their love and respect.

In all honesty, I had my doubts about Caesar's ability to lead the country at first. He opted to rule without a vice-president, making him the first president in the nation's history to do so. But throughout his short time in office, he proved to be an extremely competent president. Probably, one of the most capable leaders the nation has seen in a while. Caesar ensured to surround himself with some experienced advisors and with their help, Caesar was remarkably effective in getting things done for the people. Within the first few months of Caesar's young administration, he was able to make education more accessible, devise a way to make healthcare more affordable, and was he able to implement a community improvement project that brought well-needed resources and other upgrades to most of San Diamo's most downtrodden communities. Life was improving in the country and the people seemed happier.

Being Caesar's bodyguard provided me with an exclusive front-row seat to all the daily duties of the president. I've accompanied him to his meetings, watched him sign bills, and protected him in public when he decides to grace the people with his presence among other things. It was a difficult job, but a respectable one, nonetheless. With the increased income I was making, I was able to purchase a brand-new house in a much nicer neighborhood, one which Eliza and the children truly love. Who would've thought that a simple farm boy from Capacha would be working for the president? My life has surely changed for the better in the past few months, and it is all thanks to President Caesar.

Mr. Santiago had sent a letter to congress five months ago announcing his retirement due to his illness. It is unfortunate, yet respectable. Members of Viper received promotions as well. Hector was promoted from corporal to colonel, a position that was denied to him under the previous administration due to his protest of the reduced salaries. Speaking of army salaries, Caesar signed a bill that would increase the pay of all military members, and as a bonus, entitled them to free healthcare and other benefits.

Mr. Borgias gained a position in Caesar's administration as head of the treasury and Mr. Ambrose served as press secretary. I was unsure what had happened to the other members, but I'm sure that wherever they are, they are enjoying the fruits of their labor. One might argue that it was unethical for Caesar to give these promotions based on association instead of merit. In my eyes, however, that was not the case. This was simply Caesar strategically placing the chess pieces on the board in the best places to assure his success. Which is what any leader does.

Of course, not everyone warmly welcomed Caesar's sudden rise to power with open arms. He was able to ruffle a few feathers and make a few enemies during his brief time in office. One was a famous journalist named Javier Delgado, who was unafraid of attacking Caesar with brazen criticism on a near-daily basis, and Congressman Lucas Casano who was one of Caesar's most vocal opponents in the political ring. I suppose you cannot make everyone happy in this world, and unfortunately, not everyone will see the good in your actions. Though, I suppose constructive criticism is only healthy in a democracy.

October 15, 1984. It was a cool afternoon and I stood in the yard of the presidential mansion by a black sedan cruiser waiting for Caesar. I was supposed to drive him to an important event at the mayor's office. I waited by the car for fifteen minutes then finally, Caesar exited the mansion looking upstanding as usual. I gave my friend a warm greeting and he proceeded to open the rear passenger door to enter the vehicle before I made my way to the driver's seat. Caesar never made it a habit to have doors opened for him. You can say it was a humble charm of his. The last time I had done this he looked at me with a smile and said 'I am the president, not a king. I'll open my doors for myself.' He was truly a man of the people because he lived like the people.

During our afternoon cruise, something had crossed my mind. Just what exactly happened to Viper now that Caesar was president? Our meetings had ceased and there hasn't been a word from them ever since the revolution. Not even Caesar himself talked much about the group anymore. Of course, there would be no need for them since the main goal of removing DeOrtiz had been achieved, but perhaps it would be fitting if Caesar could do a nice gesture and give some form of presidential recognition to the group that liberated San Diamo.

"Caesar, what happened to Viper?" I inquired.

"Before taking office I restructured the group to operate in the form of an undercover government agency," he responded while reading through some important documents. "I would like for Viper to remain discreet. They'll be San Diamo's own C.I.A so to speak."

I was intrigued by this idea. I suppose an intelligence group would serve the country well in the future, but I was curious to know why establishing one was so important to Caesar. The country was more secure under his rule so perhaps having Viper work as an undercover intelligence group was working quite well after all.

"Juan, I'm going to need you for later tonight as well after the event at the mayor's office has ended," Caesar informed me.

"Do you have another meeting scheduled then?" I replied

"Something like that. I have something important to attend to in Brando,"

Brando is a small fishing town along the Rio Grande River that's just four miles south of Tipedre. I agreed to take him there. Usually, he would disclose to me the nature of some of his meetings and events for sake of his security, but he didn't do so this time, and when this happens that sent the message that whatever it is that Caesar had to attend to was highly confidential, therefore, I'd respect his privacy.

We arrived at the mayor's office an hour before the event began. Caesar was attending a meeting with all the nation's governors and other delegates today and I had a feeling that a meeting such as this would last for a while. I escorted Caesar to the meeting room and waited outside the door. The meeting lasted for two hours, a period that felt like an insufferable lifetime for me. The meeting finally ended at around 6:00 PM. Caesar stepped out of the meeting room visibly fatigued from his lengthy discussion.

"We have no more time to waste Juan, let's make our way down to Brando at once," he implored while making his way out of the building.

He was in quite the rush to make it to Brando on time. I briskly followed him to the car and got it started so that we could make our way there. The night sky began to set in as we made our way to the town. Brando was a humble place. When we arrived in the town the people all gathered by the roadside in front of their homes and shops in jubilation to watch as the president's cruiser passed by. Some of the children even chased the car as we went along our way. There were so many people gathered in the town's narrow streets to get a glimpse of their president that driving became somewhat difficult in an effort to avoid an accident. As I drove and glanced out the window to observe Caesar's adoring supporters, I felt a great sense of pride. Brando was a community that suffered from extreme poverty and to see the hope that Caesar brought to these people gave a feeling of fulfillment. It was almost as if they saw him as royalty, and that, to me, made his life all the more valuable to protect.

It was now 7:30 PM and the stary covers of the night sky had blanketed San Diamo. Our stroll through Brando came to an end on the grounds of an abandoned steel factory. A large caravan of the town's residents had followed us to the premises where I saw a group of five soldiers standing guard at its gates. They allowed our cruiser to pass then immediately closed the gates and began ordering the citizens to return to their homes at once to keep them from going any further. I began to ask myself, why Caesar would want to come to a place such as this? It didn't seem very 'presidential' in my opinion. I was highly skeptical of this, the last time I saw Caesar and soldiers in the same area it was quite distasteful, to say the least. But I tamed my suspicions and went along with what was happening.

Caesar and I disembarked from the vehicle and were then escorted to the entrance of the factory. When we came to the door, we were halted by two soldiers. How strange. Why would they stop the president and his bodyguard from entering the building?

"Show them your tattoo Juan," Caesar told me.

Without another word, I immediately rolled up my right sleeve and presented the scarred viper head tattoo to the two guards. Upon verifying my identity, they allowed Caesar and I to enter the old, rusted factory floor that was almost vacant, except for pieces of abandoned equipment and scrap metal that lay on the floor as relics of its industrious past. Meanwhile, my body was covered in goosebumps. I was glad that I was present at another Viper gathering, yet I couldn't overcome the eerie feeling in my stomach. What was the purpose of this meeting and why would Caesar hold it here instead of our usual warehouse location? I couldn't stop speculating the meaning behind all this especially given what Caesar had told me earlier today. It would be a major conflict of interest if Caesar was to be seen in a place like this. I suppose I was more concerned about Caesar's integrity than anything else.

Suddenly, another man who was accompanied by two other soldiers entered the room. It was Eduardo Luciano. Tipedre's now-former Chief of Police. I watched as he greeted Caesar with a firm handshake and joked about how he was 'honored to be paid a visit by the president.'

"Did you find them all?" Caesar asked.

"Yes, we did sir. They're all here tonight," answered Eduardo. "Shall we go now?"

I followed them as they made their way up to a platform that overlooked the factory floor below. I remained silent the entire time, electing to simply observe the proceedings of this meeting as it went along. We waited on the platform for about five minutes till eventually, a group of soldiers entered the room with several other people in their custody with pillowcases over their heads and their arms tied behind their backs.

The soldiers placed each one of the detainees onto their knees and then proceeded to remove the pillowcases from over their heads. At that moment, my curiosity and suspicion instantly became a feeling

of horror. The people on their knees, who appeared terrified and confused by what was happening, were the journalist Javier Delgado,
Congressman Lucas Casana, Captain Vasquez, three of DeOrtiz's closest business associates, and perhaps most shockingly, Mr. Santiago.
They all looked beaten and tortured, visibly petrified by the thought
of what horrors would happen to them next.

"You betrayed me Caesar!" screamed Mr. Santiago at the top of his
lungs.

I looked over at Caesar. He showed absolutely no emotion at all.
He was simply cold and unresponsive. I, on the other hand, had finally
understood what was happening. Caesar didn't just transform Viper
into an agency for public or national security; he transformed it into
his secret military police force that worked strictly by his orders with
Eduardo at its head. I watched as the horror continued to unravel as
the group drew their weapons and aimed them at their prisoners. They
begged for their lives as those barrels locked in on the back of their
necks. Why was Caesar doing nothing? How could he allow something
like this to happen in his presence and do nothing as those people
begged for their lives?

I marched over and grabbed hold of him, "stop this Caesar!" I protested. "Don't do this!"

I was then struck in the back of the head by Eduardo so hard that
I fell to the ground barely able to keep consciousness. Eduardo then
planted his foot in my back and yelled 'open fire!'. The rapid barrage of
gunshots that rang out echoed off the walls of the empty room and I
was certain that they would haunt me for the rest of my life. I watched
as the blood of the victims gushed from their now cold, lifeless bodies
and washed the factory floor clean of the rust that stained it. It was
carnage. A massacre that Caesar stood by and watched knowing he
had the power to stop. Caesar had just eradicated all opposition to his
power, and I was shaken to my core.

As I began to lose conscience, Eduardo got down on one knee,
looked me in my eyes, and said, "I hoped you paid close attention. It
would be a shame if Eliza, Julio, and Maria were to lose you,"

"He's learned his lesson, Eduardo. Bring him to the car," Caesar responded as he prepared to leave the scene.

How did Eduardo know the name of my wife and children without me disclosing that to him? Their lives were now at risk, but I had no strength to fight at that moment. My heart began racing in my chest as the room began to become darker by the minute. I looked at Caesar with fear and anger. After a while, I had finally lost all consciousness. Caesar had just revealed a different side to him and from that horrific night on, I never saw Louis Caesar in the same light again.

9

TRUTH AND GOATS

WHAT IS TRUTH? IT IS a complex thing when you think deeply about it. Truth is built on the condition that whatever is being claimed as "true" is accepted and believed beyond a reasonable doubt. This acceptance can come through many forms of convincing such as persuasion, influence, the presentation of strong evidence, our biases, or maybe even propaganda. The fact of the matter is everyone lives in their own idea of truth. Everyone lives and dies by a set of beliefs and values that they hold dear. But what if those beliefs and values aren't based in what we think is reality? One thing about the idea of 'truth' and 'reality' that most people do not tend to think about is that what we believe can be easily controlled to fit a narrative or create a certain outcome. Once you come to this realization, it then leaves you to wonder if the beliefs and values you hold are truly yours or are they just the mere reflection of the thoughts of someone else.

A rumor, for example, can only spread if its messengers accept it as reality from the person who told them. But what if the evidence proves such a rumor to be false, wouldn't you then be suspicious of the motives of its fabricator? Say for the sake of argument you are told a story that you find believable, only to find out that certain key details were left out; you would then start to question the validity of the story and its teller's credibility will you not? Society walks a fine line between truth and falsehood, and the truth is needed to ensure a society thrives in harmony. And Caesar was able to manipulate this line with great effect.

It had been three days since that night in Brando. Though I had lost consciousness, I could still vividly remember the horror on the faces of the men that were brutally murdered that night under Caesar's watch. Yes, I agreed with the idea that something had to be done about DeOrtiz's supporters and sympathizers, but bloodshed was not the answer. Men like Javier Delgado and Congressman Casana were neutral participants in this fight, and Mr. Santiago was an ally. None of those men deserved to die. Caesar had blood on his hands and if he was at peace with the idea of murdering an ally, then what does that mean for other members of Viper like myself? I was shaken by the idea of what could happen, especially given the fact that the safety of my family was now at stake. Would they be caught in the crosshairs of this madness as well?

Caesar gave me a verbal warning against confronting him in the manner in which I did back at the factory. He told me that "we cannot allow our feelings to blind us". Though he kept me employed as his bodyguard, I carried out all my duties from that day forward with a heightened sense of caution and suspicion. And I believed Caesar held the same feelings towards me. It wasn't just this newfound callousness towards his perceived enemies that made Caesar so terrifying to a degree, it was his poise and intelligence that guided it. Caesar possessed tremendous foresight and he knew that these high-profile murders, if discovered, would eventually raise eyebrows across the country; something that he simply couldn't afford to happen. He had to wash his hands clean of this issue. Luckily for him, Caesar devised a strategy that could tie up his loose ends, and he knew just the person that could help him carry it out.

Since taking the role of bodyguard to the president, Caesar gave me at least three nights every week to be with my family, and tonight was one of those nights. With all the stress I've been feeling at the office since what happened in Brando it would be nice to spend time with my family and relax in our new home. As I gathered my belongings and made my departure from the mansion, I walked by Mr. Ambrose in the hallway as he was apparently making his way to Caesar's office.

"¿Cómo te va Juan?", he greeted me as he walked by.

"I'm doing well Mr. Ambrose. You have a meeting with the president I assume," I responded.

"Yes, I do. As a matter of fact, I'm running a little late so I will see you some other time,"

I never told Eliza or our children about what happened that night in Brando, nor did I mention the fact that Caesar's secret military police unit knew of their identities. Keeping this information secret was the best way to protect my family in my opinion. Eliza could see that I was deeply troubled. She could always tell when something laid heavy on my mind. However, I simply told my wife that I was exhausted from work and cuddled beside her as I laid my head down to sleep.

The following morning, I arose early to make my way to the presidential mansion for another day of work. I stepped through the front door at 7:00 AM and found our daily newspaper delivered and sitting on the dew-soaked lawn. When I opened the paper, the pleasant morning instantly transformed into one of chaos. The headline read, "Fire at Presidential Mansion. Three Bodies Found at Scene". I immediately ran to my car and raced to the mansion, praying that Caesar was not harmed.

The scene at the mansion was pure mayhem. Hundreds of people had gathered outside the gates with worried looks on their faces that expressed great concern for the well-being of their dear 'libertador'. Fire crews and other emergency responders were present, all fatigued from the work of maintaining safety and order throughout the night. My heart sank into my chest as I examined the mansion. The entire east wing was incinerated. There was no extensive external damage, but the interior of the wing was now a charred ash pile. A testament to the massive size and scale of the fire. It is amazing that the entire building wasn't destroyed. The seat of power that had stood for decades in the heart of the nation's capital was now tarnished. What could've caused this catastrophe?

True to my duties as a bodyguard, I began to look for the president to ensure his safety. I searched across the yard, but Caesar was nowhere to be found. Hopefully, he was evacuated in time and taken to a safer location. I did, however, see Mr. Ambrose addressing the press as to what had happened. Just as he was finished, I approached him.

"Ambrose, have you seen the president anywhere?" I asked in a panic.

"Calm down Juan, Caesar is safe. He's at the National Defense Office as we speak.," he reassured. "He'll be giving an address to the nation later tonight."

He then patted me twice on the shoulder and whispered in my ear, "This is all a part of the plan". Mr. Ambrose then took his leave, but I was left to wonder what exactly he meant by this being "a part of the plan". Did Caesar orchestrate the fire? It didn't make any sense, why would Caesar plan to burn his own house down?

I turned around and saw three detective officers talking to each other. I wanted to know about the three bodies that were reported to be at the scene. As the president's bodyguard, it was my duty to know all who worked at the mansion for the president's safety. Perhaps, I could aid the officers in their investigation.

"Good morning officers," I politely greeted them. "My name is Juan Santano, I am the president's bodyguard. Could you tell me about the three bodies that were found here? I know all the mansion's employees; I think it would be useful to you in your investigation."

"Yes of course," replied one of the officers. "The bodies that were found were already in body bags outside the east wing when we arrived, and they appeared to have multiple bullet wounds. The available camera footage showed three masked trespassers leaving them at the scene. We already identified the victims; they weren't employees here."

I found the officer's account was so bizarre.

"Then who were the victims?" I questioned.

"They were Congressman Lucas Casana, that journalist Javier Delgado, and former congressman Geraldo Santiago," he replied. "There was no blood at the scene either and the bodies showed signs of torture, so that means they were killed someplace else and left here. Whoever did this may have also started the fire. We fear that they may be targeting the president, sir."

I thanked the officers for their time and then went on my way. I was shocked and frightened by what I had heard. It all made sense now, this was Caesar's plan to cover up his involvement in the murders. To distract the public and to quickly gain control of the narrative, Caesar must've ordered Viper agents to set the east wing a blaze and leave the bodies of Mr. Casana, Delgado, and Santiago at the scene to make it appear as if this was a direct attack toward him. This dramatic scene, coupled with the public's undying love for Caesar would avert any suspicion toward him while at the same time grow his support. I was wholeheartedly disgusted by such a sinister plan yet, intrigued by how exactly Caesar would go about it.

I left the mansion and drove to the National Defense Office to see Caesar and to carry out my bodyguard obligations for the day. I assumed that if I were not to do so it would raise suspicions and I would be targeted by Viper. When I arrived at the office, a security guard escorted me to the meeting room where the president was. I entered the room while both he and Mr. Ambrose, who was also there, were having a discussion.

"Juan, you're just in time. Please have seat," Caesar said to me.

There was long table standing in the middle of the room. Caesar stood at the head of the table while Mr. Ambrose sat directly next to him at the left-hand side smoking a cigar. I took a seat directly across from Mr. Ambrose. I observed Caesar, there something strange about him. For the first time ever, he seemed a bit uneased as he stood over the table, sleeves rolled up with his fingers firmly planted on the wooden surface. Was he fearing that his plan would fail?

"What's the next phase of the plan Ambrose?" Caesar inquired.

"Well. Sir, the people are understandably in a state of panic at the moment," he explained with a malevolent look in eyes as he puffed his cigar. "The public loves you and are looking to you for answers. What they need right now is to not only be reassured but galvanized as well. And I have no doubt that with your remarkable oratory skills that you'll be able to accomplish that. What the people need right now, is an enemy. We need a goat."

"What do you mean by 'goat'?" Caesar questioned.

Ambrose then stood up from his chair and said, "just leave it all to me sir. I'll handle writing your address and taking care of everything else after that. All you need to do is prepare yourself for your speech tonight."

Ambrose then left the room with an overconfident look on his face and his cigar pointing to the ceiling while it sat between his teeth. This moment demonstrated just how much trust Caesar had in his media and information mastermind. Ambrose was indeed an expert in his field, but just what exactly did he mean by giving the people "an enemy" and needing a "goat"? I looked over at Caesar as he simply stared through the window with his hands behind his back. I was still horrified and disgusted by what had happened earlier and how Caesar could allow this to happen. I was also deeply conflicted. I wanted to believe in the version of Caesar who ended DeOrtiz's regime; but at the same time, I was disheartened by the version of him that I have seen over the past few days. Are those two men different or are they both one in the same?

"Caesar, what is all this?' I questioned him out of deep concern.

He continued to look through the window with his stoic stance and answered, "Flowers cannot grow near weeds Juan. This is simply us uprooting the weeds so that the new San Diamo can grow."

No Caesar, this was you covering your tracks.

A few hours had gone by. There was a tremendous feeling of anxiety that was moving through the country due to the ongoing situation. The story of the fire was the news of the day. News anchors and pundits discussed this horrific event at great lengths in what became an endless cycle of opinions from people who may hold credible views on the matter. But there was still one major question that every news channel in the country pressed at every opportunity, where was President Caesar?

Mr. Ambrose had returned to the room and handed Caesar two pieces of paper with his address to the nation written on it. Caesar spent two hours rehearsing the speech. He muttered while doing so, therefore, I was unable to hear the content of the speech clearly. This was an unordinary experience for me. I had grown accustomed to Caesar giving fiery speeches without the need for rehearsal, so to see him do this now told me that whatever was written on those sheets of paper would have a profound impact not only on this situation, but perhaps on the entire country as well. During this time, staff members at the office got to work arranging cameras, lighting, and other equipment for Caesar's primetime address to the country. It was as if I was watching an actor prepare to take the stage for a performance.

Finally, it was now 7:00 PM. The people of the nation would at long last hear the voice of their dear president as he speaks to them about the disaster that has rocked the country. The disaster that the president himself caused but, I assume he will conveniently forget to mention. I stood in a corner of the room while Mr. Ambrose controlled the camera, and Caesar sat at the head of the table getting ready to speak. The eyes of the nation were now all focused-on the president. Lights, camera, action!

"People of San Diamo, good evening," he greeted the nation. "First and foremost, allow me to apologize for my absence throughout the day. I have been busy attending to meetings with the heads of our nation's security to discuss the unspeakable travesty that has taken place today."

He went on to say, "make no mistake, what happened today was heinous, appalling, and it was a direct assault on our nation and the law and order in which we stand for. At the scene, the bodies of congressmen Casana and Santiago as well as the journalist Javier Delgado were found. According, to police they were tortured and murdered at a different location and left at the presidential mansion during the attack by those cowardly arsonists. My sincerest condolences go out to their loved ones. According to intelligence that I have received during my time here today, it has been concluded that this vicious attack on our democracy was in fact carried out by an underground anarchist group which primarily consists of members from the native Webec people group, other members of the public, and is funded by the wealthy elites in an effort to topple this administration and wage war on your freedoms. In this time, we as true patriots of San Diamo must stand together to protect what we hold dear."

Caesar vowed to bring the perpetrators from this "underground anarchist group" to justice while attempting to rally the support of the public. I stood and watched as a man whom I believed to have had impeccable integrity spoke a mouthful of lies to his millions of people. Caesar, with the aid of his propagandist Roger Ambrose distorted the line between truth and falsehood; and I feared what this meant for the future of San Diamo. When Caesar concluded his speech both he and Mr. Ambrose then proceeded to leave the room. I continued to stand in the corner reflecting on what had just occurred. The president stepped out the room first with Ambrose following behind him. I put my hand on Ambrose's shoulder to stop him before he could leave the room.

"Remind me of why you left England in the first place," I said to him.

He chuckled. "Revolutions excite me mate," he replied then left the room.

The lies and propaganda did not just stop there. With Ambrose's position as press secretary, he had connection in most of the country's media landscape and in the weeks following the fire at the presidential mansion, he used his connections in conjunction with his own private newspaper company, to publish daily attacks on ethnic Webecians and never-ending conspiracy theories about the nonexistent anarchist group that was allegedly working in the shadows to overthrow Caesar and his administration. They became the new scapegoat in Caesar's administration, so that's what Ambrose meant by 'needing goats.' One famous caricature portrayed Caesar as a boxer in a ring holding the flag of San Diamo with a Webecian man and a wealthy banker lying unconscious at his feet. The poster read, "¡abajo los anarquistas!" (Down with the anarchist!). Caesar was the hero that was fighting to keep this group from wreaking havoc and destroying the country, and that was what the people believed.

Of course, whenever there is a force that makes it their mission to pollute minds with lies and conspiracies, there will also be a force that shines the light of truth to counter them. Some members of the public and in the media pushed back against Caesar's claims and called them out for the lies that they were. Sadly, whenever this was done believers of the lie would rail against it, some in violent ways. The police would even arrest these individuals on false charges of sedition and conspiracy to commit treason; using bogus, fabricated evidence to link the truth tellers to the fake anarchists group. Something told me that these arrests were the work of Viper agents working undercover in the police. I suppose if you're going to tell a lie of this scale you might as well do what you can to make it believable.

Truth and reality can be controlled to fit a narrative or to create a certain outcome. The result of the lies, gaslighting, and scapegoating that was imposed on the people of San Diamo was detrimental. Violence against ethnic Webecian people skyrocketed. They became the subjects of brutal, hate-filled discrimination and persecution which they did nothing to deserve. In addition to this, the homes, and businesses of some of San Diamo's wealthiest individuals were vandalized or destroyed completely, and trust amongst the people deteriorated almost overnight over suspicion of who might be involved in the unnamed anarchist group. The people were divided amongst themselves, but united behind one man: Caesar. No one in San Diamo was acting on thoughts that truly belonged to them. They were relentlessly brainwashed and had their love for the man who improved their lives manipulated for the sole purpose of procuring more power for him. It's common for leaders to lie, and it's one thing when they win the hearts of their people; but it is another thing when those lies gives you control of their minds. So again, I ask, what is truth?

10

MONEY AND POWER

MONEY, IT'S WHAT MAKES THE world go around. They say that things only have as much power as you allow them to have and isn't it rather remarkable how much power mankind has given to such simple pieces of paper. The more of it you have then the more likely you are to live comfortably in a thriving lifestyle however, the less of it you possess, the more likely you are to suffer. Money has the potential to build and to destroy, to improve lives and to ruin them, to clean and to corrupt, to give power, and to take it away. The human obsession with wealth is as old as the existence of the world itself. When it comes to politics, money has been a driving force behind the decisions of leaders ever since the days of kings. But what if money itself isn't what truly "makes the world go around"? What if instead, it is the people who control it?

It has been one year since Caesar has taken office. There have been good and successful moments in the time since the revolution, and of course, there have been quite a few troublesome ones. The east wing of the presidential mansion was nearing complete reconstruction. There were many historical memorabilia that were destroyed in the fire.

Treasures of San Diamo's past that have now sadly been lost to time and never to be seen again. However, it is nice to see the mansion be restored to its former grandeur, though I still get knots in my stomach when I remember the circumstances that caused the fire in the first place.

I was still highly conflicted when it came to Caesar. On one hand he still demonstrated his love for the common people of San Diamo and worked tirelessly to make their lives better, but on the other hand the murders, the cover ups, and the undercover Viper agents that were in all facets of the government and the public made me question his integrity quite a bit. Is a good deed still good if the means by which you do it are dreadful? Can a person still be considered good if they've done awful things? I wanted to believe in the man that I met at that warehouse a year ago, and in some ways I still did. However, they say seeing is believing, and given what I've seen; I'm unsure of what to believe. At this point, Caesar has committed acts that not even DeOrtiz himself had done in his time. I just hope that he won't continue to spiral down this dark path.

Today is June 8, 1985. Things have been relatively normal ever since Caesar's fiery cover-up operation, that is of course if you choose to simply ignore the lingering fallout from the controversy. Ethnic Webecians were still the victims of detestable acts of discrimination, and public hysteria over who may and may not be involved in the made-up anarchist movement was still a contagious disease, one that even infected the halls of congress itself. Yet, Caesar carried on his duties as president as if nothing had ever happened, and the country followed his lead.

It was just another afternoon in the office. I stood behind the president as he sat at his desk reading and signing through a ginormous mountain of paperwork. I most definitely wouldn't be able to do a job such as that. Suddenly, there was a knock on the office door.

"Please open the door Juan," Caesar requested of me.

I did as he asked, then entered the former bank owner turned Head of the Treasury, Mr. Raul Borgias who was accompanied by two other well-dressed men as well as two mansion security guards. I dismissed the guards, closed the door, then returned to my place behind Caesar's desk.

'It's been a while since I've seen you Mr. President," Borgias said as he and his associates took a seat in front of Caesar's desk.

"Much too long indeed mi amigo," Caesar replied. "I'm happy you could make it; we have much to discuss."

"It's good to see you as well Santano," Borgias greeted me. I simply gave him a nod in return.

My concerns were growing over this abrupt meeting. It would seem that whenever Caesar is in the company of a person who bore the viper head tattoo something horrible happened. My heart was earnestly praying that this wasn't one of those times. Caesar took out a binder from one of his desk drawers and handed it to Borgias.

"That is the funding proposal for the new railroads project that I want to present to congress next week," Caesar explained. "As usual I need your approval on the final spending amount before I move forward."

Borgias took out a cigar from the inner pocket of his blazer and began smoking it as he examined the contents of the proposal. He gently nodded his head as a sign of how impressed he was then locked his cigar in between his fingers when he was finished.

"This is a rather interesting proposal Mr. President," he acknowledged. "Thirty-five million is quite a large amount, but I'd be more than happy to approve it; on one condition."

"And what might that be?" the president asked.

Borgias slowly took another draw of his cigar and released a large puff of smoke into the air.

"As you know, with my new position as Head of Treasury, I can't be involved directly with of my business," Borgias elaborated. "These two men are associates of mine that I've put in charge of my business while I'm away serving. This is Mr. Costa and Mr. Alonso. Two weeks ago, I sent them to broker a deal to purchase a shipping company that operates out of the port. The owner, however, was being rather 'uncooperative'. It's a shame that he doesn't know that I have friends in high places."

"What do you mean Borgias?" Caesar replied with a tone of suspicion.

"What I mean Mr. President is that we're in a position of 'help me – help you'. I want this business under my control, and I would like Viper's help in doing so. You send agents to get Mr. Parilla to cooperate and I'll approve the proposal. You get what you want and so will I. Everyone wins."

Caesar sat forward in his chair staring blankly into space as he tapped his fingers on the desk, pondering the unexpected circumstances he was now thrust into.

"Is this really the position you want to put me in Borgias?" Caesar asked as he looked at him with a dour expression on his face.

Borgias stared back at him, smoking his cigar with a stolid look on his. "Perhaps you've forgotten who betrayed DeOrtiz and funded your little revolution that has you sitting in that chair right now."

The room grew tense as both men were now locked in a power struggle. The unscrupulous negotiation now turned into a staring contest between Caesar and his own Head of Treasury. Finally, in a matter of minutes, Caesar conceded and agreed to help Borgias acquire the shipping company within two days on the condition that he immediately approved the funding proposal upon its completion. Borgias and his associates obliged to the terms, then arose from their seats and prepared to leave the office.

"It's always a pleasure to do business with you Mr. President," Borgias taunted before exiting the room.

Caesar then sat back in his chair. Glancing into space with a look of utter disgust on his face and gave a deep sigh.

"I despise that man," he faintly whispered while shaking his head.

Never had I ever seen Caesar fold to anyone. It was a truly unprecedented moment, and one that was deeply troubling. I could tell Caesar was reluctant to give in to Borgia's demands. However, Caesar's entire rise to success hinged on the financial resource that Borgias provided.

I would never look at Caesar and say he holds fear in his heart for any man. That would seem illogical to me, I'm not even sure if Caesar possessed the ability to feel fear. Therefore, when it came to Mr. Borgias, Caesar saw the method of appeasement as his best strategy. Like a parent who spoils their child by giving them whatever they desire when they cry for it. Although, I did begin to question who actually held the power based on this situation. Perhaps that's the reason why Caesar despised Borgias so much.

"Juan," he then called out to me. "You have yet to prove that you're still trustworthy ever since that night in Brando. I want you to go on this mission tomorrow night. Make sure that you get Mr. Parilla to cooperate."

There I was, now a pawn in Caesar's chess game with Borgias. Caesar had good intentions by wanting to secure the funds for the railroads project, but I was deeply unhappy with his request. I wanted no part whatsoever in this extortion plot, especially given what I've seen over the past year. I did not know Mr. Parilla let alone have any quarrels of my own with him. Yet, I was chosen to do the work in order to please Caesar's oversized financier. I internally protested this decision, but for the sake of my family I accepted the task. Caesar ordered me to return to his office tomorrow night for further instructions. I only hope that my hands won't be stained with blood when this is all said and done.

The next night I returned to the mansion and walked through its magnificent white hallways to Caesar's office. I entered the office and found Hector present there as well, comfortably sitting in a chair and having a drink with the president.

"Well, if it isn't the president's bodyguard," Hector said with his rough voice as I entered the room.

"Its good to see you as well Hector," I replied sarcastically as I took a seat next to him.

"Would you like a drink Juan?" Caesar offered me.

I politely declined, then Caesar opened his desk drawer and placed two folders onto the desk. Hector and I each picked up one from the table and began reading what was inside. There was a picture of a man as well as three sheets of paper filled with detailed information, a picture of floor plan, and what appeared to be a contract.

"Tonight, both of you will go to the home of Mr. Winston Parilla," Caesar instructed. "He is the owner of "Envio Continental" (Continental Shipping), one of the largest cargo carriers on the continent. He lives in a suburban town called Huertos which is just five miles north of here. Get him to sign the contract that is inside your folders and return here when it is done."

"Juan," he then continued. "Hector will be accompanying you tonight. He's already devised a plan. All you need to do is follow his lead and don't do anything foolish."

I looked Caesar into his eyes and simply nodded my head. Hector and I were then dismissed, and we both exited the mansion without saying a word to each other. We decided to use my car to go to Huertos, a hillside community which was home to some of San Diamo's most wealthy families. I heard that massive, luxurious mansions lined almost every square-inch of that town. The wealthy elites sitting in their castles on their hill looking down on the peasants below. Thankfully, the power in Tipedre doesn't work for them anymore.

It took us two and a half hours for us to reach Huertos. The rumors were true, the town was packed with massive mansions, as well as exotic cars within the driveways of every home, freshly trimmed lawns and beautiful gardens, clean streets, and tall palms trees that tied it all together with a charming aesthetic. I never knew a community of such affluence as this existed in San Diamo. This only served as evidence that within this one country, people lived in two vastly different worlds.

It was now 9:35 PM. As we drove through the community, Hector read Mr. Parilla's address to me once more. 235 Pinewood Street. It took another five minutes before we arrived at the location. I was mesmerized by what I saw. A pearly white masterpiece of modern contemporary architecture that was sealed off by a huge gate with two guards keeping watch standing before me across the street. It personified the exorbitant wealth that Mr. Parilla possessed. As I prepared to exit the vehicle, Hector grabbed my hand.

"Wait. We'll move in when the lights go out," he said.

He then gave a slight nod to the security guards standing by the gate to which the guards returned in kind. They were Viper agents, so this was Hector's plan. We sat and waited in the car for nearly three hours. It was 11:55 PM. Hector sat in the car smoking a cigarette while I sat quietly looking out the window.

"Are you convinced now Santano?" Hector asked me.

"Convinced about what?"

He took another draw of his cigarette as he gave a blank gaze through the windshield.

"Just look around. Just look at these houses, this community," he expounded. "These people are some of the richest in all of San Diamo. They had the power to help change lives and make the country better for all but instead they kept it all to themselves and focused only on making themselves richer while the rest of us just rotted away. I know you're an idealist and you question some of Caesar's methods; but if you had the power, would you let your ideals stop you from doing the right thing no matter the cost?"

This was most humane I've ever seen Hector behave. His question was no doubt very thought-provoking and pushed me into a brief moment of soul searching. The moment was cut short however, when a cover of thick darkness fell over our location. It was now midnight and the lights in Mr. Parilla's house were now off.

"Time to go," said Hector as he threw away his cigarette and handed me a flashlight.

Hector and I then exited the vehicle and slowly approached the gates of the house. The two undercover Viper agents posing as the security guards opened the gates to allow us into the yard. We then used our flashlights to maneuver our way through the pitch-black darkness that surrounded us. Given how dark it was, Hector must've ordered one of the agents to cut the house's power supply. We then approached the front door and stood in formation as if we were performing a military breach. Hector placed his flashlight in between his teeth then proceeded to skillfully pick the door's lock so we could enter the house. Upon entering, we heard what sounded like two individuals in a scuffle.

"Let me go!" a voice yelled in the darkness.

"Turn the lights on," Hector ordered.

The lights then suddenly returned and illuminated the luxuriously decorated Mediterranean styled interior, furnished with granite countertops, marble tile flooring, white leather couch seating, taxidermy, a fireplace, and a crystal chandelier in the ceiling. Mr. Parilla was then thrown down to the floor of the living room where we were all gathered by another Viper agent who must've entered through the back door.

"This is a lovely home Mr. Parilla," Hector said as he sat comfortably on the couch.

"Grab me something nice to drink," he then ordered one of the other men.

Mr. Parilla sat on the floor visibly shaken by what was happening.

"Who are you people?" he stuttered.

"Calm down Parilla," Hector said as he received a glass of wine. "We're businessmen. We're just here to do business with you."

"What do you want? I have money. Lots of money. Just take whatever you want."

Hector took a sip of his wine, "I would love your money Mr. Parilla. But, unfortunately, that's not what we're here for."

Hector then reached into the shirt pocket of the army uniform he was wearing and removed a piece of paper. He unfolded it slowly, it was the contract that Caesar gave to us. Hector threw the contract on the floor in front of Mr. Parilla then slowly removed a pen from his pocket.

"Some friends of ours approached you not too long ago with an offer to buy your company. They weren't too pleased with your behavior, so they sent us to do some 'convincing'. We don't want to hurt you Mr. Parilla, all we ask is that you cooperate. Take this pen, sign those papers, and we'll be on our way."

Parilla became irate. "Go to hell!" he defiantly yelled in response.

His arrogant outburst was then met with a handgun pointing at the back of his head by one of the other Viper agents. Mr. Parilla immediately became silent.

"I think you might get there first if you don't sign those papers Mr. Parilla," said Hector sarcastically before taking another sip of his wine.

Intimidated and left with no other option, Parilla slowly took the pen from Hector's hand and tearfully signed away his company. Hector then picked up the papers from off the ground.

"It was a pleasure doing business with you sir," Hector mocked as he refolded the papers and placed them back into his pocket. "We're done here."

Hector and the other men made their way out the house and I followed closely behind them. As we made our exit, the sound of sobbing caused me to stop. I turned around and watch as Mr. Parilla was left on his knees crying over what had just transpired. I began to reflect on what Hector had asked me earlier. I did have my ideals and I did believe that our actions would lead to a good cause that would inevitably benefit all of San Diamo. I despised elitist men like Mr. Parilla, but as I watched him, heartbroken and sorrowful on the floor, something in me changed. It felt wrong, and I began to feel sympathy for him. Nonetheless, I painfully turned a blind eye and walked out the room with a moral warfare taking place in my mind.

The transaction was now complete. The following day Caesar handed over the signed contract to Mr. Borgias and in return, Borgias approved the spending proposal for Caesar's railroad project. Congress debated over the project for two weeks, and when it was all said and done, it was approved in the final vote. Caesar delivered a vital resource to the people of San Diamo, but at what cost? Does stealing from the rich and giving to the poor make stealing something righteous to do? These questions, coupled with the fact that this victory was only achieved by robbing a rich and greedy man to pay another rich and equally greedy man, made this victory somewhat bitter-sweet. But I suppose that feeling is common when you play a game of money and power.

11

THEMIS

IT IS NOW DECEMBER 1985. Christmas is now fast approaching and the atmosphere in Tipedre is buzzing. It didn't snow in San Diamo but the magic of the holidays was still felt across the country as the people of San Diamo had another thing to look forward to at this time of year, Christmas Carnaval. If you weren't going to church during the holidays, then you could look forward to the massive parade celebration held every year just three days before Christmas day. A celebration where the entire city becomes the uncontested party capital of the world. Music, food, dancing, shopping, and merry making will be the order of the day in just three short weeks. Unfortunately, however, the mood in Caesar's administration during this season was anything but merry.

Caesar constructed a fortress around him that was strategically guarded by agents of Viper that hid in plain sight within most of the political and social circles of San Diamo, as well as Caesar's elite group of "specialists" that would aid him in running the country and managing some of the more difficult matters. This was how Caesar was able to maintain his grip on his power while managing the affairs of the country. Arguments could be made about the ethics of it all, but this was Caesar's way of getting results and so long as he was delivering for the people, he would have their unwavering support. The support of the people was the foundation of Caesar's fortress. About two months ago however, cracks were beginning to form in the walls of the seemingly impenetrable fortress, and through these cracks emerged a new threat to Caesar's power.

Bursting onto the scene was Alejandro Henriquez, a young, charming, energetic, and charismatic political newcomer who wasted no time in asserting himself as Caesar's rival with an appetite to bring him down. He was quite brave. Prior to this no one had the courage to challenge Caesar in any way, especially after the way he ceased power through revolution and military intimidation as opposed to the more traditional method of campaigns and ballots. But if you're going to attack a fortress, you better ensure that you have a strong enough army to do so. Luckily for Henriquez, he had his army; and they were ready to fight. We all know the old saying of "the enemy of my enemy is my friend", and Henriquez was sure to comprise his army with Caesar's enemies. He managed to garner support from the ethnic Webecian community, the wealthy elites, members of congress who secretly opposed Caesar, and quite shockingly, members of the public whose hearts weren't on board Caesar's train. Henriquez's army was small and less skilled than Caesar's, but small and less skilled armies have miraculously won wars before, haven't they? Sometimes size and skill don't matter if you are well-led and have a strong will to fight. Sometimes a small shepherd boy with a slingshot and a stone can slay a giant with sword.

Henriquez's grassroots opposition to Caesar utilized attacks such as public rallies, media interviews that attacked Caesar by exposing his short-comings and labeling him as a 'secret dictator', and members of congress opposing Caesar at every turn; something that didn't happen during the earlier months of his time in office. This message was only amplified across the country due to the support Henriquez received from wealthy pockets. With this aid, his sphere of influence grew even larger as time went by. An anti-Caesar movement was growing, and so were the rumblings about something that would put Caesar's power to a coin-flip, elections.

As expected, Caesar took notice of his new, lionhearted adversary and decided to fight back. It was suggested by Eduardo and others if Viper should 'dispose' of Henriquez, but Caesar, thankfully, chose to not do so for if Henriquez was to come to any harm or just 'mysteriously disappear', then it would easily be traced back to him and cause complications. It was a wise decision. Caesar instead elected to take a more subtle route. He decided to let Ambrose run smear campaigns in the media against Henriquez, claiming that he was a part of the anarchist group that was working to bring down Caesar and that the fire at the mansion was his idea. The plan was working, and with Henriquez's support from ethnic Webecians and the wealthy elites who have been the scapegoated subjects of hate and vitriol for over a year, it was solid evidence in the eyes of the public and support for Henriquez began to wane. That was of course until Henriquez quickly countered that narrative.

It's December 20, 1985. Last night, Henriquez somehow managed to slip through Ambrose's grip on the airwaves and took to national television from a secret location with a weapon so fatal, so explosive, so damming that it would no doubt sink Caesar's presidency in an instant and win him the war. A Viper agent had gone rogue and made an alliance with Henriquez, and on that faithful December night, everything was revealed. Henriquez announced to the entire nation that he had evidence that tied Caesar to the plot behind the fire at the presidential mansion and who was in fact responsible for the deaths of Congressmen Casana and Santiago, as well as the journalist Javier Delgado and all the other men. Henriquez brought the rogue agent on with him and used him as his trump card. The agent confessed to the entire nation that Caesar was in fact the one who orchestrated the fire at the mansion to cover-up the murders of Casana, Santiago, Delgado, and the other men. He also told them where the murders took place, and if that wasn't bad enough, he also revealed Viper's existence and explained to the entire nation that the revolution was a plot by Viper and that members were in all facets if the government and the public. He even went as far as revealing that members could be identified by the viper head tattoos on their right forearms. That night, Henriquez gave himself the nickname 'mongoose' and vowed to rid San Diamo of the vipers once and for all.

All hell had broken loose. The cracks in the walls of Caesar's fortress had now turned into huge holes. The rumblings of elections turned into calls for the president's immediate resignation. The following I, along with Hector, Borgias, Ambrose, Eduardo, and a few other Viper agents were gathered in the president's office. Caesar barged into the room and furiously wiped his desk clean of whatever was sitting on top of it. I had never seen him so angry before. The public support that he had enjoyed as a safety bed for so long had now evaporated overnight, and he was aware of it.

"Ideas. I need ideas!" he fumed.

The room sat silent for a while. Everyone exchanged simple sideways glances with one another, none of us knowing what to say in order to quell Caesar's anger.

"You need to remain calm Mr. President," Ambrose said as he broke the silence. "Maybe, we can fabricate evidence to disprove Henriquez, confuse the public, and then perhaps we wait until this all blows over until it's not a story anymore."

"No," Caesar replied. "That will turn into a 'he said-he said'. It will only be his word against mine and no one will believe me."

"Then we need to cut Henriquez out of the picture entirely," Hector suggested.

"Bloodshed will only make this worse!" the president fired back.

Caesar then stood behind his desk; his head hung down in distress and with both hands firmly planted to its surface.

"You're all useless to me right now," he said in a faint tone. "You're all dismissed. I have a better idea."

Everyone left the room without another word. I followed closely behind them but before I exited the room, I turned around once more to see just how uneased the president truly was.

"What are you going to do Caesar?" I asked.

He gently nodded his head. "Human beings become dangerous whenever they're in three states Juan. When they're in a state of silence, when they're in a state of anger, and when they're in a state of desperation," he responded.

"Which one are you in right now?" I replied.

"Desperation," he answered as he looked at me.

Without another word, I closed the door and left the room. Caesar was right, people are dangerous when they feel desperate. My concern for what Caesar might do in his desperation grew with each passing minute. He had endless options available to him. When people are in a state of desperation it can lead them to all sorts of madness; or maybe, it can cause them to look for divine intervention.

There is a law that is written in San Diamo's constitution that is called Article 5. Under this law, during a state of 'grave national crisis', congress will be dissolved, and all functions of the government suspended as all power is then concentrated to the president. A form of emergency powers if you will. This law, however, can only be enacted and ceased by the nation's most powerful judge, the Head of the High Court. The High Court consists of three judges that are responsible for giving rulings on some of the nation's most controversial matters. This law has never been enacted before in San Diamo's history, and with no clear definition of what a 'grave national crisis' is, this law can become lethal if weaponized. You would be a fool to think that Caesar didn't have someone with this kind of power at his disposal.

During the revolution, the former High Court judges were arrested, never to retake their positions on the bench. Many people saw them as an ineffective bunch that only served DeOrtiz, so no wonder they drew the ire of Viper. Following Caesar's rise to power, three new judges were placed on the court which meant there was a new Head of the High Court, a position that only went to the most experienced of the three judges. And the new Head of the High Court was none other than Ms. Claudia Paulo.

The next day I drove to the presidential mansion for another day of work. The crisp cool December morning breeze contrasted the great tension that was in the air. Christmas was now four days away and Christmas Carnaval was tomorrow night. At this time of year, the streets of Tipedre would be filled will with people going shopping and enjoying the pre-Carnaval festivities. However, given the dire situation that has unfolded, the mood in the city was far less jolly to welcome the holiday. I arrived at the mansion to witness it's gates being swarmed by peaceful protesters with placards who were demanding that Caesar step-down from office immediately. Soldiers stood outside the gates to keep them from advancing beyond that point.

I made my way into the mansion through the rear gate. I eventually came to the front steps of the mansion and made my way inside. Upon my entry, I saw the hallways flooded by media crews who were patiently waiting in front of an empty podium. I made my way through the crowd and proceeded to Caesar's office. Given the circumstances, something told me that an announcement of seismic proportions would've been made. As I approached the door of Caesar's office, both he and Ms. Paulo exited and began walking in my direction. Apparently, they were making their way to address the press.

"It's good to see you again Juan," she said to me with a smile as she walked by.

"It all changes today my friend," Caesar said as he did the same.

I said nothing to them as went down the hallway. This was a bizarre moment, and that was exactly why it was so discomforting. Ms. Paulo was there the night of the revolution's planning. She was more of a 'sleeper agent'. She never spoke much since I've known her, she merely carried out her daily duties on the High Court in a manner that disguised her involvement with Viper. Honestly, I had forgotten that she was a member at all. She was like a relative that mostly distances themself from the family but only shows their face during special occasions. So, for what purpose would Caesar need the Head of the High Court to be present? Was he going to announce his resignation and announce Ms. Paulo as his successor? Was he going to agree to take on Henriquez in an election? Caesar did say he was in a state of desperation; and it is always wise to be aware whenever someone feels cornered.

I followed them both back towards where the media crews were and when we arrived, I simply stood in a corner, laser focused on what was about to occur. Ms. Paulo then made her way to the podium and gave the announcement that rocked San Diamo to its core.

"Ladies and gentlemen, good afternoon," she welcomed. "I wish my being here today was under better circumstances. Sadly, we stand on the precipice of a moment of an unprecedented national crisis, one that after much deliberation with the president, has brought me here to perform my most sacred duty."

"People of San Diamo, our nation is under attack by anarchists who want to bring down our country," she continued. "We cannot allow that to happen. These anarchists are spreading poisonous, and incendiary lies that will undoubtedly tear the country apart at its fabric. According to our intelligence officials there are rumblings of a civil war brewing in our great nation. We cannot allow this to happen. Therefore, I, Head High Court Judge Claudia Paulo with the power invested in me under the San Diamo charter; hereby invokes the power of Article 5. Indefinitely."

The reporters then instantly unleashed a barrage of questions aimed at Paulo. I wanted to believe that my eyes were lying to me. Anyone with common sense could see through this illusion of 'national crisis' that was being displayed. Paulo's soliloquy of lies just ushered in a new era in San Diamo. Caesar, in a desperate bid to secure his position as president, had just consolidated all power in the country into his hands. And there was no one who could stand in his way. A modern day acquiring of absolute power.

Louis Caesar then took to the podium to address the nation for the first time, not as its president; but as San Diamo's new dictator.

"People of San Diamo, I would like to urge you all to not be alarmed," he said. "Our security as a nation is paramount in my mind. We cannot let these anarchists and their leader Alejandro Henriquez take our control. We must work together to ensure our nation's safety and to begin this process and to avert any immediate dangers, I hereby impose a state of emergency. A nationwide 7 PM curfew tomorrow night. Therefore, this year's Christmas Carnaval is now cancelled."

Just like that, the pride and joy of San Diamo's festivities had been wiped away. There was no doubt that this decision would be deeply unpopular, I'd be surprised if the people didn't gather in their thousands to protest this decision. My intuition told me that Caesar's time as San Diamo's leader would now be entering a dreadful phase which would lead to a horrific end. For now, however, the most joyful time of the year was greeted by what only felt like an ocean of fear that was washing over the country and drowning the people with paranoia of the uncertain future that awaited. Christmas this year would begin with a silent night.

12

IRON FIST

IT IS NOW JANUARY 1986. The calm and collected version of Caesar that I had met nearly two years ago at that warehouse was now a paranoid individual who saw enemies everywhere. The man that promised to bring San Diamo into an era of peace and unity had now divided and conquered it. He made quick work of showcasing his now limitless power. His use of Viper for example, was no longer restricted to its conservative, undercover methods. Instead, Caesar opted to let the presence of his beast be known and allow Viper to conduct large scale arrests of his presumed enemies with Eduardo in charge. There was no time wasted in ensuring that Henriquez and that rogue agent who revealed Caesar's secrets to the nation were taken away and no one in knows if they are dead or alive. Caesar also ensured that the media was under his thumb. With Ambrose's help along with that of the military, Caesar made an aggressive effort to censor any reporting that was deemed unfavorable to him and jail any journalist who dared to oppose him. If all this wasn't enough, Caesar still had his public agents and his committed supporters in the public who worked on his behalf to crush any form of dissent and turn in those who didn't support the great 'libertador'. This was a new San Diamo, one that didn't belong to the people but to the ambitions of one man.

Those who feared this new autocratic regime packed their belongings and made an exodus across the borders into neighboring countries that were willing to take them in. Eliza begged me to leave Viper and abandon this madness. I agreed with her, but unfortunately, I couldn't bring myself to do so for the sake of protecting her and our children. I was still concerned that they may still be under Viper's radar. Instead, I decided that her and the children leave Tipedre and go to Capacha. With the increased uncertainty, it would be best if they stay as far away from the city as possible. For some time, it was apparent that Caesar was the undisputed leader of San Diamo. There was no one to challenge his authority. No congress, no Henriquez, no opposing media group, absolutely no one. Or at least that's what I thought.

Football, or soccer as it is called in other parts of the world; was like a second religion here in San Diamo. Whenever there is a match of any size, be it a local community game or a big college one, hundreds of people come out in droves to enjoy the action. Football was a way of life here. I remember as a child when I would play in the streets with some of my friends and pretend to be Pele himself. Those were simpler times back then. Today is January 14, 1986, and this afternoon there will be an international friendly match that will be played between the San Diamo men's national team and the visiting Mexican men's national team at the San Diamo Stadium located in the town of Sevilla just 5 miles east of Tipedre. It is expected that the stadium will be filled at capacity with 50,000 adoring fans from across the country ready to cheer on the home team. To make this game even more special in a sense, Caesar himself would be in attendance.

Caesar knew that by taking absolute control of the country, he had made numerous amounts of powerful enemies that salivated over the idea of taking him down one way or the other. He feared the idea that someone would do to him what he did to DeOrtiz, or maybe they'll do worse. To ensure his safety, Caesar expanded his security team. I was no longer the only Viper agent tasked with guarding the president's life, and for an event such as this, I'm almost glad that I wasn't. Caesar did, however, keep me as his closest guard out of fear that some more rogue agents might be hiding in his new security group. With this being the case, I was the only one in his security team that was allowed to personally drive his cruiser while the others followed in a motorcade. The motorcade had its perks, we never had to deal with traffic so we were able to arrive at the stadium with ease and cut the long lines to enter the stadium's VIP area at the north end entrance where Caesar would watch the game. Of course, our only setbacks were the loyal supporters at the stadium who swarmed us just so they could shake hands with the man who they could see no faults in.

The VIP area of the stadium was a suite at the top of the north section that was furnished with its own bar, lounge furnishing, food catering, and private restroom. Accommodations that were fit for a celebrity. Caesar and I took a seat in one of the couches while the other bodyguards surrounded us with two standing at the sides and at the rear. After about an hour or so, the stadium was filled to maximum capacity and the thunderous roars of the hometown fans grew louder by the minute as they eagerly waited to watch their home team play. This was perhaps the most relaxed I've ever been since joining Caesar's presidency, it was also the most relaxed I've ever seen Caesar behave. To be honest, I was unsure if everyone present at the stadium were simply trying to distract themselves form Caesar's dictatorship or if they were just completely oblivious.

The energy in the stadium was electric as both sides went back and forth. You'd be forgiven if you mistook the match for a championship final instead of a mere meaningless international friendly. Halftime had come and the score was locked at one-a-piece. The high tempo energy in the stadium had simmered a bit as the teams made their way into their respective locker rooms to devise their game winning strategies. During this time however, there was a slight change in the wind. I detected some ominous presence in the room. I remained seated in the couch next to Caesar and began to observe the room to find what was triggering my suspicions. It was just me, the president, the other bodyguards, and a few of the stadium's employees who were working at the suite's various amenities that were present in the room It all seemed quite normal. Except, for one suspicious figure, the janitor. I couldn't explain why, but something about the seemingly harmless young man who was minding his business and mopping the floor provoked my intuitions. Due to this, I gaged my focus on him.

Caesar then tapped me on the shoulder. "Can you please grab me a drink from the bar?" he requested of me.

I arose from the couch and made my way over to the bar to request a bottle of beer from the bartender. As I stood at the counter waiting to receive the drink, I continued to focus my attention at the janitor. He looked to be in his early twenties and was simply trying to make an honest living. What was it about this baby-faced man that caused me great concern? I probably was just being paranoid, maybe even a little envious of the fact that the days when I looked so young and handsome were slowly drifting behind me. The bartender handed me the drink that Caesar had requested and as I made my way back to the couch where he was sitting; the young janitor made his way behind the two guards protecting Caesar's rear, slowly lifted the shirt of his uniform, and quickly drew a handgun from the waist of his pants. I immediately dropped the beer and sprinted to Caesar as fast as I could.

"Get down!" I screamed at the top of my lungs.

I quickly grabbed hold of Caesar and brought him to the ground just before the assassin in janitor's clothing fired three rounds towards him. The other bodyguards that were present immediately drew their weapons and returned fire. The shots echoed throughout the stadium and sent all who were there to enjoy a pleasant afternoon of football into a frenzy of people who scrambling for safety. Caesar and I were helped to our feet by the other guards. Both I and the other guards then promptly proceeded to escort Caesar out of the stadium for fear of his safety. The assassin was shot multiple times in the chest by the guards and laid on the floor in a pool of blood gasping for air. One of the other guards was also wounded in the mayhem. Caesar took the injured guard's gun then ordered another guard to stay and help nurse his injury. Afterwards, we proceeded to follow the remaining body-guards who also had their weapons drawn through the chaotic stadium corridors. My heart was racing, and my face was dripping with sweat as we attempted to get to safety. Another threat could come from any time from any corner and at this moment, no one could be trusted. Caesar moved with great haste, obviously anxious to return to the presidential mansion and yet, he didn't show a look of fear or worry on his face. He was president on the outside, but the soldier in him was clearly still alive. In all honesty, I found the threat of another assassin a bit less terrifying than what was probably going through Caesar's mind.

As we made our daring escape, the other guards ordered the stam-peding people out of our way; they even went to more forceful mea-sures such as simply pushing people out the way. During the ordeal, we came to a door that led to a stairwell. We decided to use the stairwell as a shortcut out of the stadium. While making our way down the flights of the stairs, another assassin dressed as a security guard ran into us as he came up the stairs with his gun drawn. He fired two shots at us when we entered his sight, one of which struck another guard in his stomach. I quickly ducked for cover, but Caesar stood tall and returned a single shot at the assassin. The bullet struck the attacker in his shoul-der, causing him to drop his weapon and roll down the steps in agony. Apparently, Caesar didn't need bodyguards after all.

I picked up the wounded guard and carried him down the rest of the stairs. We stood over the wounded assassin as he groaned in an-guish at our feet. It was another young man who seemed to be in his early twenties just like the first assassin.

"I want him arrested," Caesar ordered.

The last standing guard that was with us then proceeded to ap-prehend the assassin as Caesar, and I made our way to the cruiser. We didn't experience another attack and when we made our way outside, I gave the injured guard over some other guards who were standing outside by our vehicles. Caesar and I then quickly ran into our cruiser as we sped off alongside a smaller motorcade. Caesar and I returned to the sanctuary of the presidential mansion unscathed from the frightening attack. Caesar wore his usual poised demeanor but as I looked into his eyes as we made our way to his office, I could tell they burned with a vengeful passion. He took a seat behind his desk and gazed at the ceiling with a deathlike silence. A chill began to run through my body over the thought of what was running through Caesar's mind.

"Come here Juan," he ordered.

I walked over to Caesar and stood before him at his desk. He then stood up and gave me a hug.

"Thank you for saving my life today mi hermano," he said to me. "Go home and get some rest now."

"No Caesar. We don't know if the threat is still looming. I think it is best if I stay here with you to ensure your protection tonight."

My adamance to stay with Caesar to protect him was just a disguise. The truth is I decided to stay with him only to see what his next course of action would be. It seemed that every time he sent me home for the night, he would carry out some maniacal plan by morning, and I was determined to break that pattern.

"Very well then," Caesar agreed. "Contact Ambrose. Tell him I need to make an announcement."

I did as he asked and contacted Ambrose who wasted no time in arriving to the mansion with a camera crew. Caesar was preparing to give a primetime address to the nation. While the camera crews were setting the stage for Caesar's address, I began to think about the assassin that was taken into custody. Was that young man now in Brando lying dead? Were there more assassin's just like him and if so, who were they and when will the next attack be? All these questions raced through my mind, but it was clear to me that the attempts on Caesar's life were done out of the growing anger that some felt towards his decision to become the all-powerful dictator of San Diamo. The opposition against him had now resorted to violent measures, and I had no doubt in my mind that Caesar would respond in kind. After thirty minutes, the camera crew had finished arranging the equipment for Caesar's speech.

"Good evening my fellow Diamans," Caesar opened his speech. "Thank you all for your time. Today, during the friendly football match at the San Diamo Stadium, an unspeakable and horrendous attempt was made on my life by two assassins."

"For those of you who were present at the stadium today, I do wish to extend my apologies for any inconveniences and feelings of fear that this attack had brought to you," he continued. "I wish for you all to know that thanks to the remarkable bravery of my security team, I am well. Unfortunately, two of my bodyguards were injured in the attack, but they are currently nursing their injuries in hospital, and they are expected to make a full recovery. One of the assailants was killed in the attack and another was wounded and taken into custody. But make no mistake, this failed foolish attempt by these anarchists will be met with harsh retribution. I vow to hunt down each and every last one of these traitors and rid San Diamo of this scourge once and for all."

I stood by the office door as Caesar gave his speech, his strong rhetoric sent a clear message. If that wasn't bad enough, he also announced a nationwide lockdown that would be in immediate effect. This meant citizens could carry on with their daily lives by day but under increased military supervision and must return to their homes by a set time at night. It also meant that all means of travel both within and from the country were now suspended until the lockdown was lifted. Caesar now tightened his grip on the entire country. Fortunately for him, everyone now believed his lies about the anarchist movement that was plotting to take him down; unfortunately for the people, his lies were now reality, and they all had a target painted on their backs.

The next morning, I packed up my things and decided to make my way home. I had spent the night at the mansion to observe the president even further. Thankfully, he didn't do anything dramatic in any way for the rest of the night. Following his address to the nation he went to bed without another word. As I made my way home however, my attention was drawn to a large crowd that was gathered outside of a park in downtown Tipedre. I pulled over to see what the commotion was about. When I had finally shuffled my way to the front of the crowd, I was horrified by what I saw. It was almost as if I was standing in the medieval era. Makeshift gallows with the bodies of the captured young assassin and the rogue agent who announced the existence of Viper to the nation swaying in the wind with a sign that read "los traidores serán castigados" (traitors will be punished") above them. A public hanging, how sickening. This was Caesar's message to the nation; no longer would he be conservative with his power, but he will assert it without mercy and destroy those who stood in his way. No more would he be the leader with the gentle hand, but the ruler with an iron fist.

13

"THEN I WILL"

TWO WEEKS HAVE NOW PASSED since the assassination attempts. During that time, life in San Diamo was like being in a
maximum-security prison with zero hope of escape. Where guards
patrolled the streets around the clock and the warden of the prison answered to no one. The borders were closed, only shipping vessels that
were coming into the country were allowed passage and all its cargo
were heavily inspected by soldiers. Airlines were also now restricted
to transporting non-citizens to their home countries but keep all citizens grounded. You couldn't even drive into another province. Caesar
had restricted the movements of the people and began an aggressive
campaign to root out all the suspected anarchists from the country.
Hundreds of innocent people were arrested by Viper agents under
false accusations of their involvement in plots to bring Caesar down.
I've heard many of them were taken away to undisclosed locations
and subjected to brutal methods of torture to extract confessions, and
with the courts on Caesar's side; many of these individuals were sent to
prison by way of bogus, unfair trials. That was of course if they were
lucky. Though Caesar did still do his best to improve the lives of average

citizens, the dark side of his presidency was a paranoia fueled witch-trial meant to terrorize the very same people he was helping.

Caesar rewarded me the Medal of Valor, an honor only given to citizens who display remarkable acts of bravery. It was my reward for saving his life during the attacks but knowing what the man who gave this award to me has become; the piece of silver was like coal in my eyes. It's a bitter-sweet trophy if you asked me. At this point, I have become even more conflicted about Caesar's true nature. He provided hope for the San Diamo common folk and for that; he was beloved even to this day by a considerable section of the population. However, he was also deeply hated for his actions and made plenty of enemies from every corner of the country. I stood by him out of my continued belief in his ability to improve the lives of the less fortunate but distanced myself from him due to my growing mistrust.

I woke up early to a day that was dimmed by the blanket of grey clouds in the sky. My home has been silent ever since I sent away my family. There was nothing but the sounds of soldiers who had just finished their nightly patrols going by my house. The loyal foot soldiers heading home after a long night of acting on the instructions of their mad king. As I yawned my way out of bed and rubbed my tired eyes on the way to the kitchen, I found an envelope suspiciously sitting on the table. How strange. I didn't leave this letter here, so who did? There was no name or address written on it. I sat at the table and began to slowly open the envelope. There was a single folded piece of paper inside which I removed. It read, "meet me at the cathedral tonight". I was stuck thinking to myself who could've sent this mysterious invitation, as well as if I should accept it or not. After some time pondering, I decided that I would go to meet the letter's unknown sender.

I didn't go to the mansion that day, I decided that it would be best to get away from the drama for a while and think about what the best course of action in the future would be. Should I take the risk of resigning as Caesar's bodyguard and maybe become a target for Viper? I was close to Caesar and therefore I knew all his secrets, given the current situation, along with Caesar's now oversuspicious mindset; that may not be the best thing to do. Plus, any attempts to talk Caesar out of his madness would be futile at this point, so what was I to do?

After spending hours contemplating my options in the solitude of my home, I noticed that it was almost time for me to make my journey to the cathedral for my meeting with the secret host. It was now 7:15 PM and the curfew had already begun. To make my travel a lot easier, I chose to shed my skin as Caesar's bodyguard and reemerge as a soldier in the San Diamo army. I had stored my old uniform away in my bedroom closet, I never thought I would ever have to put it on again but for the sake of ensuring my safety and easy maneuvering through the tight security in the city, I decided that it would come in handy tonight. I looked in the mirror when I finished dressing, and all I saw was the reflection of a man wearing the uniform of an oppressive past on the outside; but was now plagued with uncertainty about its future on the inside. Maybe tonight I would find my answer as to what must be done. Maybe this was God leading me towards a much-needed answer, so in a sense it's fitting that I would have to go to the cathedral. I placed my hat on my head, picked up my handgun then made my way out the door.

The security of the nightly patrol was suffocating. I had passed three checkpoints on my way into Tipedre and Viper agents were present in almost every corner of the city that I drove by. There was no one else present in the city that night. Tipedre was just a pit of venomous snakes that no one dared to go close to. I parked my car in an alleyway that was just three city blocks away from the square where the cathedral was and decided to make the rest of the journey on foot, blending in with the rest of the agents in soldier clothing. As I came into the square, the memories began to flood my mind. This was where it all began. That night two years ago. A day that went from with the disorienting sounds of flashbang explosion from battling angry protestors in the streets, to staring down the barrel of Hector's gun on the cathedral steps, to finally becoming a member of Caesar's secret organization. Things have changed a great deal since then, and they were about to change once again.

I entered the yard of the cathedral and admired the statue of the Virgin Mary once again, this time without saying a word. I then proceeded to make my way up the steps of the old building, then slowly made my way inside with my gun pointing in front of me. Inside the cathedral was mostly dark with only the shimmer of the moonlight shining through the old stained glassed windows working as a light source. The massive congregation hall was mostly lifeless, except for a woman with long black hair sitting quiet and alone at the end of one of the benches in the front row. I slowly walked up the carpeted center aisle as I approached her with my weapon drawn, ready to squeeze the trigger in an instant.

"The bible said those who live by the sword will die by the sword Juan," the woman said with an awfully familiar voice as I drew closer to her.

"Or maybe that doesn't apply to you anymore since you and Caesar started playing God," she continued as she rose to her feet.

The woman slowly turned around. It was Mesilinda wearing her famous black hood. I brought my weapon down in disbelief. She looked much older, but something about her was different. I saw a tremendous amount of pain and anger in her eyes. She looked as if she had suffered a great loss of some kind.

"It is good to see you again Mesilinda," I said to her. "How are you doing? Did you find your father?"

"The feeling isn't mutual Juan," she fired back at me. "You have no right to ask me about my family right now."

She then, with tears in her eyes, took a seat in one of the benches. I was had no words for her nor could I think of a way to console her. I have never seen her cry before, inside the ferocious tigress was a heartbroken cub with nowhere to go. My heart ached for her.

"Were you the one who sent me that letter?" I asked.

"I did," she sobbed. "You're the only person I can trust right now."

I stood silent as Mesilinda began to ease her sorrow. I watched as she closed her eyes and held tightly to a necklace of a crucified Jesus that she was wearing around her neck.

"My father died while in prison," she said as the last drops of tears fell from her eyes. "He got sick, and he didn't make it."

The look of sadness on her face then turned into one of pure fury.

"And they were my brothers," she continued in a tone mixed with pain and anger. "Those two assassins that tried to kill Caesar, they were my older brothers."

I was blown away by her shocking admission.

"Your brothers tried to kill Caesar!?" I shouted in belief.

"Their names were Diego and Alberto," she replied. "They were all I had when our father was in prison. Diego was the one that was killed at the stadium, and Alberto was the one that was hanged. Caesar hanged my brother!"

She then looked at me, rage in her eyes and tears going down her cheeks. "He has to pay for this, and you're the only one close enough to him to do it," she hissed at me.

I couldn't believe her suggestion. I understood her anger and felt her pain. Anyone would burn with a similar vengeance if their loved one died in a similar fashion. Unfortunately, I was still torn. I agreed that what Caesar has done was awful, but to take his life; that was a different matter. He brought hope to San Diamo, and to take away that hope in the name of vengeance would be a greater crime in my opinion.

"I understand your pain Mesilinda, and I'm truly sorry to hear what has happened to your family," I replied in an attempt to quench her wrath. "But Caesar is a good man, and he is bringing hope to the people. We can't just take that away from those who support him. Besides your brothers tried to kill him knowing they were outnumbered."

Mesilinda immediately rose to her feet in a fit of rage and slapped me across my face for my insult to her brothers.

"He's a mad man Juan! Can't you see that!?" she yelled at me. "People saw hope in DeOrtiz and look at how he turned out. My brothers were only doing the right thing and don't you dare disrespect them. You know I am right Juan; you've seen it for yourself. Don't let whatever faith you have in him blind you from that fact."

She then took two steps closer to me till her were now standing chest-to-chest and eye-to-eye.

"You are the only person who can do this Juan," she said to me with a soft tone "More will suffer if Caesar doesn't go. You always believed in doing the right thing, I know you do. Consider that scar on your tattoo as your resignation."

She then drew even closer to me and gave a sharp death-stare into my eyes.

"If you don't have the courage to do what's right, then I will," she warned.

Mesilinda then shrugged me aside and furiously strutted out of the cathedral. I was left with no words, only a more conflicted mind over the thought of killing a man I've grown so close to, and even more shaken by the threat that Mesilinda would do it herself if I didn't. I sat down in one of the benches, rolled up my right sleeve, and stared at the scar on my arm as I thought about what Mesilinda had just said. I then slouched on the bench and look at a large painting of the crucifixion of Jesus Christ that hung on high on the wall behind the pulpit.

"Lord help me," was all I could say as I sat alone in the cathedral desiring divine direction for what I should do next.

14

BLOOD AND DUTY

ONLY A FEW SAYINGS IN life are truer than the old, simple proverb of 'what goes around, comes around'. Irony is one of the most comical things in the world, and it is also one of the most revealing. It is now February 1986, and Caesar had now become the victim of his own creation. His isolation of the wealthy business class forced them into retaliation. Those who had the ability to do so, ended their business operations in the country, instead opting to work in other countries. Within the past few weeks, some of the largest and most successful companies in the country left for greener pastures and hundreds of thousands of people lost their jobs overnight. With no work to pay any wages so people could survive, plus everyday essential resources now becoming scarce; the blame now laid solely at the feet of one man. The people that once saw Caesar as their savior would turn against him. That, along with many people in the country being outright fed up with Caesar's dictatorship that was becoming increasingly brutal as the days went by, created the perfect storm for what would happen in Tipedre on that faithful day. Oh, how things have come full circle.

The mob fury which began the ending days of DeOrtiz's time in office two years ago had now returned to exact its justice against Caesar. However, this was not like what it was back then. Insanity, and violence swept through the streets of the capital city that morning like a gust of wind blowing across a grassy plain. Caesar had used every tool at his disposal to ensure the security of his presidency. Up until this point he has not shied away from using Viper to undertake methods such as intimidation, lies, threats, exploitation, imprisoning his challengers, and of course, murder as ways to maintain his stranglehold on power. By resorting to these methods over the past two years, he was able to eliminate his opponents while simultaneously using smoke and mirrors to consolidate the support of the people that his power hinged upon. But things have changed greatly over the past year and Caesar was now in a state of survival. So, what do you do when you find yourself in a state of survival? You could run, or maybe; you could fight. Those are the two options available to you, and with his support now dwindling before his very eyes, Caesar chose the latter; and unleashed his beast onto his own people.

February 17, 1986. I returned to my bodyguard duties at the presidential mansion at 7:00 AM on that oddly warm morning, just three hours before the carnage that day unfolded. It started off as a rather relaxed and slow day at the presidential mansion, nothing exciting in any way to speak of. The other employees at the mansions went about their duties as usual and the city streets were still heavily patrolled by Viper soldiers as it had been for the past month. I sat alone in a chair in Caesar's office. The president, or should I say, dictator; was in another room attending to a meeting with some of his associates in the army. It amazes me how anyone still found peace in their conscience to still work with Caesar given everything he's done, let alone be in the same room as him. I suppose that sometimes loyalty to power is stronger than morals, but who am I to judge when I'm still guarding Caesar's life? In all honesty, that was where my inner conflict lied, though mine was less out of loyalty to the power and more to belief in the cause. But was this a cause still worth believing in if I couldn't even recognize its purpose anymore? I joined Viper that night so I could make a positive, but now I'm unsure if I've accomplished that at all.

As I sat slouched in the chair watching the time tick by, my mind went back to that night in the cathedral with Mesilinda. I understood her pain, but to kill Caesar, that was something I just couldn't bring myself to do. Knowing her threat to do it herself if I failed to, made me ask myself if I was truly doing my duty as bodyguard by not warning Caesar. Loyalty to Caesar or ending his reign of terror, what was the right choice? My moment of thought however, was interrupted by the smell of tear gas and what sounded like gunshots and a massive brawl coming from the hallway. I immediately got to my feet and began walking to the door to find out what the commotion was about till suddenly, the office door flew open and in came one of the mansion's security guards.

"Where's the president?" he asked as he tried to catch his breath.

"He's in the meeting room. What's going on?" I replied.

"The mansion is under sieged," he answered. "Some protesters have breached, and soldiers are holding them back. We must evacuate now!"

I immediately ran out of the office behind the other guard to make my way to the meeting room to find Caesar. I couldn't believe what I saw in the hallways, angry rioters fighting with soldiers, police, and mansion security guards as they stormed the mansion. The putrid and disorienting scent of the tear gas caused my mind to travel back to when I stood on the frontlines two years ago fighting to defend the mansion and my own life during the last riot. However, this was unlike what happened back then. The anger being expressed by the rioters was so intense that its heat filled the room, and, perhaps most terrifyingly; some of the soldiers opened fire. A few of the protesters were mercilessly gunned down, and this only stirred the anger of the rioters even more. The halls of such a prestigious building had now become a battlefield stained with the blood of the very same people it was built to represent. What a nightmare.

Making my way to the meeting room became a struggle as my eyes burned and breathing became difficult from the tear gas that was being used. I ran up the stairs heading to the west wing of the mansion and looked out the windows as I passed by, I was in utter shock by what was happening outside. Hundreds of protesters were storming the mansion's grounds. Scaling the fences and battling with soldiers and law enforcement with all kinds of weapons as they attempted to make their way into the mansion. There was no doubt in my mind, Caesar's sins had now caught up to him, and the people were determined to have his head for it. Their beloved liberator had now become their oppressor.

The situation was escalating quickly, and finding Caesar became an even greater priority with every passing minute. When I finally arrived at the meeting room, the army officials that were in the meeting with Caesar were already being evacuated by members of the mansion's security, but there was no sign of Caesar.

"Where's the president?" I stopped one of the guards to ask.

"He was just evacuated. His motorcade is getting ready to leave from the south gate," the guard replied.

There was no time to waste. I began sprinting through the hallways as fast as I could to get to the south gate before the motorcade left. Inside the mansion was in utter panic as the staff members raced through the halls to find secure locations to hide and soldiers marched in to help provide reinforcements to lift the siege. I had never seen anything like this before, and something told me that what was to happen in the months to come would be equally, if not; more frightening. I arrived at the south gate's location to find security guards entering their vehicles to escort Caesar to safety and soldiers outside the gate doing their best to clear a path for the motorcade by using tear gas and flash bangs to disperse the angry mob that had gathered outside. There were six cars ready, and it appeared that the car that Caesar and I normally used together was occupied by another guard with Caesar in the back seat. The first five vehicles in the motorcade were ready to go, and that left the last car at the rear waiting for me to take the wheel. I quickly ran down the stairs and got into the car, bracing myself for the daring escape we were about to make. Afterwards, two soldiers opened the south gate and we sped off into the city in a desperate attempt to protect Caesar from the very people who once loved and admired him.

For the second time in a month, Caesar's life was on the line, and he had to be rushed away to safety. A testament to just how hated he has truly become in recent times. As we raced through the city, my heart broke from what I saw. Tipedre had become a warzone. The city streets were in a state of unrestricted chaos as Caesar's heavily armed Viper agents in military gear clashed with the mostly plainly dressed and inexperienced rioters, some of whom brought heavy weaponry of their own. Some of the people fled for cover out as they were ruthlessly attacked by a barrage of tear gas and flash bangs. The clashes were fierce, and it felt as if the very fabric of the country was being torn apart. If that wasn't horrifying enough, some of the soldiers fired live rounds at the crowds. Some of the rioters were ruthlessly gunned down, and the streets of the Tipedre, the shining metropolis of San Diamo; was stained with the blood its people. I briefly began to wonder if Mesilinda was the mastermind of all this carnage as a way to avenge her brothers. It was unlikely, but very possible.

The motorcade was moving towards the northwest section of the city, and judging by the familiar landmarks, we were moving towards the Fort Mendez Military Base outside the city. We would have to get to the highway before crossing the Rio Grande Bridge. What were Caesar's thoughts about all this? How would he respond? Would he make an example out of all the apprehended rioters and hold a mass public hanging? Or would he put their heads on spikes outside the presidential mansion? Whatever it may be, I knew it would be an atrocity. As we made our way to the highway, my vehicle came under heavy gunfire. Our motorcade was spotted by some of the rioters who was following behind us in a small truck, and what started as an emergency evacuation now turned into a high-speed chase through the city. The rioters wanted Caesar by any means necessary, even if that meant hunting him down.

"We need to move! Pick up the pace!" I screamed into my walkie talkie.

We began drifting, swerving, and racing at high speeds to escape our assailants that were somehow able to keep up with our every move. The rear windshield of my vehicle was destroyed by the gunfire. Some of the other guards within the motorcade returned fire in order to deter the attackers but to no avail. I could feel my heart thumping in my chest and the rush of adrenaline coursing through my veins as sweat poured down my face amid the action. We were nearing the highway and with no other option of evasive maneuvers left at our disposal, I was left with no other choice but to put my life in the line so that Caesar and the rest of the motorcade could escape.

"The rest of you go," I said over the walkie talkie. "I'll hold them off.'"

A few of the other guards and Caesar himself tried to talk me out of my decision, but I wasn't convinced. I was prepared to die for my country and die for the cause of Caesar's crusade. I knew I wouldn't die a hero because some would hate me for my sacrifice while others would love me for it. I would be more of a martyr than a hero. I told the other drivers to speed up, and we approached the straightaway that led to the highway. Once the rest of the motorcade was far enough ahead of me; I turned my vehicle around, the road pavement marled with the skid marks of the car's tire tracks. I then took a deep breath and asked the Lord to forgive me, and with my mind now at peace with choosing death, I charged my vehicle at full speed towards the pick-up truck that our attackers were in.

I came under heavy gunfire as I raced like a charging bull the attackers with no intention of stopping or moving out the way. As the two vehicles inched closer and closer, I glimpsed the scar across the viper head tattoo on my arm one more time, and I immediately began to second guess my decision. Was Mesilinda right, and if she is, am I about to die for the wrong reason? This, along with the thoughts of how heartbroken my family would be and memories of time as a young child in Capacha swept through my mind. Time slowed down within those last few seconds before collision. I turned the wheel as quickly as I could, taking a last second opportunity to swerve the car out of the way of the oncoming truck, but I failed. The two vehicles collided with each other with a force so powerful that both the car I was in, and the pick-up truck began to roll in opposite directions like two balls of mangled mental. The truck made a direct hit with the driver side of my vehicle, it felt as if my soul left my body as I was violently tossed back and forth, and I was left in utterly excruciating pain. If it had not been for that last second turn, I attempted, I would probably been dead. Or maybe it was a miracle that kept me alive.

My car was turned onto its roof after the crash. It felt as I had broken every bone in my left arm and had a few broken ribs, and that made the struggle of climbing out of the wreckage more difficult. It took me awhile, but after a minute or two I was able to climb out of the car and get to my feet. Blood was dripping from my forehead, and I sprained my left ankle in the collision as well, so even standing became harder. I looked over at the wreckage from the pick-up truck and saw three bodies surrounding it. None of the attackers survived. Their blood was now on my hands, a memory I'll have to live with forever. I then turned my eyes up the street to see the highway in the distance, Caesar and the others had escaped. I saved them and knowing that I did was a bittersweet feeling. I began to limp away from the scene. My body was damaged, but my mind suffered the most damage from the frightening near death encounter.

As I moved back towards to city to find a place to rest, I was stopped in my tracks by the sound of someone charging behind me from out of an alleyway. I turned around quickly to see a young man wearing a red handkerchief mask around his mouth, brandishing a pocketknife running towards me. It was kill or be killed, and without any hesitation, I quickly drew my handgun and opened fire at my attacker. One. Two. Three. That was the number of shots that I fired into the chest of the young man who now laid at my feet bleeding to death. But as I looked at the young man as he squirmed in anguish and nearing his last breath, my body went cold. He hesitated when he saw my face, as if I looked familiar to him. As matter of fact, those dark brown eyes that screamed with agony looked familiar to me as well. I began to tremble as I looked over at the pocketknife that he had in his hand. I read the words that were carved into its wooden handle, "blood and duty". No, it couldn't be. I fell to my knees and slowly removed the handkerchief covering the young boy's face, and as the tears began to run down my face; I wish I hadn't. I now wish I had died in the car crash because if I did, he would've lived. Julio, my own son, laid dead in my arms. I murdered my only son. In doing my duty to protect Caesar, I failed in my duty to protect my son. Blood and duty, "a man must always stand up for what we know in his heart is right". That's what I told Julio on his birthday. And as I sat weeping with my dead son in my arms, my broken finally decided what was the right thing to do.

15

MARCH 15ᵀᴴ

MARCH 15ᵀᴴ, 1986. THE FIFTEENTH of March is a very important date in history. Firstly, it is the day we celebrate San Diamo's independence. The day when the people of this great country come together to remember the end of tyranny and oppression from our colonial past. The day when we stand united to commemorate the birth of liberty in our borders. The occasion is truly a remarkable one. However, there was nothing joyous or unifying about this special day. The country was divided, a cracked piece of glass just waiting for another stone to be thrown before it could finally shatter into a million pieces and be free from its fragility. It felt as if everyone was holding their breath as they walked on eggshells. There was no sense of freedom, nor trust, nor a common belief in unity; all that existed now was Caesar's iron regime, and rumors of a civil war to put an end to it.

Yes, that was how far down the bottomless hole of madness the country had fallen into. It was now tethering on the edge of a war between brothers and sisters, a far cry from the safety of the collective joy we all felt when DeOrtiz was finally removed. Oh, how much have things changed in such a short time. How quickly peace and hope turn into violence and pessimism. Proof, that nothing in this life is set in stone. Peace, hope, even life itself, all these things come to an end. This is a lesson that I learnt the hard way in a deeply personal fashion.

In the weeks following that faithful day, one that I wish I could forget; I avoided all contact with Caesar and Viper as a whole. At this point, they may be thinking that I had died. Ironically, on a deeper level, I was dead. I was nursing my physical injuries from the car crash, and I was healing quite well, but I had to come to terms that the deep mental and emotional wounds I suffered would never heal. I fell into an endless pit of depression and alcohol became the only thing that could soothe me as I mindlessly believed in the illusion of it taking the pain of my grief away. For a few moments it would, but after waking up from my drunken dreams, I would always be left with the chronically painful memory of the haunting echoes of those three bullets and my disdain for my own reflection. I had become a shell of my former self. The reflection of a bushy bearded man, with soulless eyes, and no purpose. Only the agony of my guilt was recognizable to me. I had spoken to Eliza two nights ago over the phone. During our conversation she told me that Julio went to Tipedre and asked if I had seen him. She told me that before he left Capacha, he was railing against Caesar, and he wanted to be a part of bringing him to justice as he would often recite what I had told him about blood and duty. I didn't have the heart to tell her what had happened to our son. How could I? All I could do was abruptly end the call, and wallow in tears as I felt proud of my son for doing what he thought was right in his heart. He was more of a man than I could ever hope to be.

Also, in the weeks prior to that faithful day; Louis took his powers to a new, and shockingly more frightening level. Throughout this entire time Louis had been patient, refusing to use the full extent of his power and finding enough mercy to provide warnings against threatening his power. Even if those warnings were horrendous in their delivery. It is often advised that you must never poke a sleeping bear, and you must also never provoke a venomous snake. Louis had run out of patience and had now decided to remove the gloves. He implemented a brutal and indiscriminate crackdown on his perceived enemies. Within the past few weeks, Viper had made several arrests of the riot's leaders and organizers including those who were accused if being involved in the riot, even if there was no evidence to prove these allegations. Hundreds of people from across the country were either unjustly executed or imprisoned. Louis was no longer concerned with doing governing for the people. He had become drunken with power. At times I couldn't tell which was stronger, my alcohol, or his lust for more control.

March 15th is also significant for another reason, as it is also the day when Julius Caesar, war hero and dictator of the Roman Empire died. Twenty-three stab wounds from some of the most important men within his inner circle was how one of the greatest and most renowned leaders in the history of mankind met his end. As I sat on the roof of the five-story apartment building in the cool of the spring afternoon observing my scarred viper tattoo, I began to reminisce on the past two years. I reflected on how life was under DeOrtiz, how I came to join Viper, how I was enamored by Louis, and how my faith in him held strong even through his veil acts. I remembered what Hector had said to me that night in Huertos, I remembered what Mesilinda said to me that night in the cathedral, and most painfully; I remembered watching Julio's life leave his body. All these memories have brought me to this day, and my mind was now made up.

I sat on that roof overlooking the park across the street. A bottle of gin in my right hand and a Carcano Mod 91/38 rifle sitting by my left. I was careful not to drink too much that day, I needed my vision to be perfect. Distanced shooting was something that I excelled in during my army training, and I was going to put those skills to the test for perhaps the last time. It was just after one PM in the afternoon, and according to my intel, the target would be at the Independence Day event that would be held in the park that was set to begin at two o'clock. It wouldn't be long now. The conditions were perfect. The sun was beaming down, and the wind gently moved through the city, greeting everyone and everything in its path with a soft kiss. As I cleaned the lens of the rifle's scope, I observed the park across the street. Thankfully, the trees wouldn't obstruct my vision. I could see where the target was expected to be so clearly that it would make a blind man envious. I made one final check on my ammo. Three rounds, three chances. That was all I had, and I had to make them count. Now that my inspection was complete, all I had to do was wait.

As the time slowly ticked by, I watched as the park slowly began to fill with people who came out to celebrate the day's festivities. Within that park which was draped at every corner with the national colors, were hundreds of people going about their day not knowing what was to come. In just a few short minutes they would all be running and screaming in panic, but for now, let them enjoy themselves. Afterall, ignorance is bliss. The roof that I was standing on was adjacent to the stage platform that was assembled in the park. I was growing evermore anxious with each passing minute and my trigger finger was beginning to itch. So, to pass the time, I watched some of the cultural performances that were happening on the stage the below to help ease my mind. It's funny, those performances meant something once upon a time, and maybe soon, they would mean nothing. Who would've thought that San Diamo would get to this point? Maybe, in some poetically nuanced way, I wasn't going to carry out my plan for myself alone, but for San Diamo as well. Maybe, just maybe, I would be saving the country from the evil that was to come. As if I wasn't already convinced, I had just found another strong reason to reassure my motives.

It was now 1:50 PM, and the people in the park began to flock towards the large metal framed stage sitting perfectly in the center of the park. The target had arrived just five minutes before. Excellent, everything was the falling into place. The rabbit had now entered the eagle's sight, but it wasn't quite time for the mighty bird to swoop down on its prey. I grabbed my rifle and sat still on the roof while keeping a close eye on the target, waiting patiently for the right moment to strike. The air grew thicker with each passing minute, this was a decision of monumental proportions. But nothing was going to turn me away now. It had to be done. I took a few more sips of gin to calm my nerves, till I was then interrupted by the sound of thunderous cheering and applause coming from the park.

The target was now moving towards the stage. It was time to do what needed to be done. I took one last sip of my gin. I picked up my rifle and with one eye open as I looked through the scope, began to set my sights on my prey. The target went onto the stage and waved to the adoring supporters who came out in droves to bear witness. A shocking site to see, but don't worry, their adoration will come to a miserable end soon. The target stood behind a podium on the stage and prepared to give a speech, I knelt at the edge of the roof preparing to take my shot.

I took one more sip of gin before once again gazing through the rifle's scope to lock in on the target before taking my shot. This was it, the moment of truth. There was no turning back now. The target had began speaking to the audience. Steadying my nerve became difficult as thoughts of Julio began to flood my mind. Eventually, the cheeks began to flood with tears as this happened. I wiped the tears from my eyes, then proceeded to carry on with the plan. A gentle gust of wind brushed through my hair and my skin became plagued with goosebumps. I took one more deep breath, then finally, with no more mental reservation; I pulled the trigger. And in that moment, time slowed down as the bullet whistled through the air, on its way to greet the target with a kiss of death. One shot, one shot was all it took. In a matter of seconds, the bullet hand travelled from the nozzle of my weapon to the side of the target's head. In almost cinematic fashion, I watched as that single bullet viciously penetrated the target's skull, sending brain matter and blood flying in every direction imaginable, and the audience that came to see the target fleeing the scene in a mad stampede. At last, justice had been brought. There was no possible way, unless by some divine miracle, could the target had survived. Those who were with the target ran to provide immediate aid, but I knew they wouldn't succeed. As for what would happen to me next, well, it didn't really matter to me. I was just pleased that it was finally over. I was just pleased that Caesar was now dead.

Printed in the United States
by Baker & Taylor Publisher Services